EMPOWERED 2022

WORDS OF POWER

Edited By Allie Jones

First published in Great Britain in 2022 by:

YoungWriters®
Est. 1991

Young Writers
Remus House
Coltsfoot Drive
Peterborough
PE2 9BF
Telephone: 01733 890066
Website: www.youngwriters.co.uk

All Rights Reserved
Book Design by Ashley Janson
© Copyright Contributors 2022
Softback ISBN 978-1-83928-644-5

Printed and bound in the UK by BookPrintingUK
Website: www.bookprintinguk.com
YB0520C

⭐ FOREWORD ⭐

Since 1991, here at Young Writers we have celebrated the awesome power of creative writing, especially in young adults where it can serve as a vital method of expressing their emotions and views about the world around them. In every poem we see the effort and thought that each student published in this book has put into their work and by creating this anthology we hope to encourage them further with the ultimate goal of sparking a life-long love of writing.

Our latest competition for secondary school students, Empowered, challenged young writers to consider what was important to them. We wanted to give them a voice, the chance to express themselves freely and honestly, something which is so important for these young adults to feel confident and listened to. They could give an opinion, share a memory, consider a dilemma, impart advice or simply write about something they love. There were no restrictions on style or subject so you will find an anthology brimming with a variety of poetic styles and topics. We hope you find it as absorbing as we have.

We encourage young writers to express themselves and address subjects that matter to them, which sometimes means writing about sensitive or contentious topics. If you have been affected by any issues raised in this book, details on where to find help can be found at
www.youngwriters.co.uk/info/other/contact-lines

✫ CONTENTS ✫

Independent Entries

Doctor Cheese — 1

All Saints Catholic College, Huddersfield

Isaac Fitzpatrick (13) — 4

Beech Hall School, Tytherington

Thane Davenport (13) — 5
Charlie Barnes (15) — 6
Amelia Semp (15) — 8
Daniyal Muhammad (16) — 9
Harold Ghorbanian (15) — 10
Joel Wilson (15) — 11
Luke Francis (15) — 12

Birkenhead High School Academy, Prenton

Katie Bragg (14) — 13
Bethany Cullen (14) — 14
Bethany Moran (13) — 16
Charlotte Hilder (14) — 18
Katrina Skiba (13) — 20
Phoebe Fielding (14) — 22
Ava Seabury (14) — 24
Philippa Davies (14) — 25
Taylor Lewis (14) — 26
Holly Wade (14) — 27
Villie Newman (14) — 28
Awen Kingsley (14) — 29
Ava Ryan (14) — 30
Teesha White (14) — 31
Ava Morrissey (14) — 32

Fatima Miller (14) — 33
Ella Gardner (14) — 34
Bonnie Lovell (14) — 35
Molly Mason (13) — 36
Seren Hulse (14) — 37
Emilee Crossley (13) — 38
Phoebe Lewis (14) — 39
Niamh Cull (14) — 40
Becky Wan (14) — 41
Isobel Goodier (14) — 42
Lauren Hayes (14) — 43
Olivia Baker (14) — 44

Chatham Grammar School, Chatham

Alexis Brown (13) — 45
Deborah Adelaja (12) — 46

Chessbrook Education Support Centre, Watford

Ollie Jokkrathok (13) — 48
Jack Jokkrathok (13) — 50
Harmonie Lord (12) — 51
Ricardo Da Costa (14) — 52
Lucas O'Connell (13) — 53
Marcus Stipa (13) — 54
Asim Babar (13) — 55
Bradley Hill (13) — 56
Oliver Priolo Walker (13) — 57

De Warenne Academy, Conisbrough

Niamh Ackroyd — 58

Lewis Cox	60
Courtney Frost (13)	61
Jessica Johnson	62
Hadassa Nkoue (11)	63
Minnie Jackson (12)	64

Dwr-Y-Felin Comprehensive School, Neath

Rebecca Rubin (14)	65
Lily Williams (13)	66
Daria Nita (14)	69
Jennifer Matthews (14)	70
Saul Otteson	73
Sophia Mead (14)	74
Lily Mandale	76
Megan Cross	78
Logan Lacey	80

Fulwood Academy, Fulwood

Eva Callaghan (12)	81
Benjamin Fargher (11)	82
Bouthaina Boutaine (12)	83
Emily Bradshaw-Allen (11)	84
Mohammad Taqi (12)	85
Yuvraj Singh (11)	86

Heathfield Community College, Heathfield

Oliver Brewer (15)	87
Alice Cronin (15)	88
Ellie Pascall (15)	90
Aneshka Hunter (15)	92
Owain Roberts (15)	94
Izzy Hearsey (13) & Leila Wort (13)	95

Hungerhill School, Edenthorpe

Ethan Buckley	97
Yu Qing Huang	98
Ameenah Din (12)	100
Chloe Nesbitt (13)	102

Mia Wilson (13)	104
Lilly Ryan	105
Kacey Compton (12)	106
Grace Hobbs	107
Ashlea Rawlings (15)	108
Sasha Lilly	109
Riley Lowcock	110

Kingsford Community School, Beckton

Anna Kwan (11)	111
Thuvaragan Yogeswaran (15)	112
Shafiqar Namuwaya (12)	114
Gracie Steward (12)	116
Gabija Surovec (14)	118
Aisha Salim (12)	119
Obinna Azu (14)	120
Arpita Hossain (12)	121
Nazmia Njie (15)	122
Sheka Hamdoun (13)	123
Kiril Kazakov (12)	124
Rajveena Kaur (12)	125
Daniel King (12)	126
Yannick Castro (13)	127
Iris Bagga (12)	128
Taqrim Arabi (13)	129

Lathom High School, Skelmersdale

Scarlett-Jane Hart (14)	130
Emily Clegg (15)	131
Jessica Morgan (13)	132
Millie Evans (14)	134

Marriotts School, Stevenage

Rashed Hussain (14)	135
Phoebe Henry-Beattie (16)	136
Emily Bartosik (13)	138
Oscar Gonsalves (17)	140
Lexi Morley (12)	141
Cleo Iftime (11)	142

Sky Newman (14)	143
Tiana-May Redford (14)	144
Riley Dale (14)	145
Jessica Parker (14)	146
Lauretta Sylvester (14)	147
Theo Milburn (12)	148

North East Surrey Secondary Short Stay Unit, Hersham

Oliver Goodenough (15)	149
Freddy Johnson (16)	150
Emilia Wall (13)	152
Kenny Campbell-Smith (14)	153
Harrison Gianni (14)	154
Nathan Brown (13)	155
Sophie Robinson (14)	156

Orion Academy, Blackbird Leys

Jack Pearson (15)	157
Caden Watts (15)	158

Outwood Academy Ripon, Ripon

Lola M	160
Ruby Fielding (12)	162
Jasmin W D (13)	164
Ashley Collins (12)	166
Myles Wainwright-Baker (13)	167
Shaneequa Aryee (13)	168

Plume, Maldon's Community Academy, Maldon

Olivia Jayawardana (13)	169
Harrison Monk (12)	170
Lois Kingsford (14)	172
Paddy O'Brien (14)	173
Molly Welsted (15)	174

Poltair School, St Austell

Rihanna Williams (11)	175
Lill Durham (12)	176

Lucas Hart (12)	177
Jacob Wells (11)	178
Rhianna Smith (14)	179
Phoebe Jones (13)	180
Ellie-May Hockaday (11)	181
Molly Wharmby (12)	182
Hollie Wheat (12)	183
Anastasija Truskovska (13)	184
Grace Quinn (12)	185
Chloe Owen-Walmsley (12)	186
Leah Rapson (12)	187
Lilly Morcom (12)	188
Jack Stanhope (12)	189
Klea-Ava Spiller (11)	190

Sgoil Lionacleit, Isle Of Benbecula

Neil MacRury (12)	191
Allan Smith (13)	192
Patricia MacDonald (13)	194
Erin Steele (13)	195
Naomi Menzies (12)	196

St Peter's Catholic School, Surrey

Aston Wong (15)	197
Conor O'Riordan (14)	198
Veronica Delgado Barrios (15)	199

Taunton School, Taunton

Julian Rampaul	200
Ema Petkova	201
Carlton Chu (14)	202
Tom Middleton (14)	203

THE POEMS

Respect LGBTQ+

Strolling in the park is a peaceful pastime.
It can also be a romantic place.
You turn the corner and see two girls kissing.
Is this a dare? What else are you missing?
They laugh and look so happy,
Until a group of boys surround and mock them.
The boys spit at them and start hissing.
How do the two go on living?

Have you ever seen that one person that everyone wants to date?
A guy with the best hair or the girl with the prettiest face?
Because everyone is expected to love right?
Don't assume society has the best insight.
They feel like an outcast because they were told they had to love
But in reality, they just want to be single.
When they reject people they try to be polite.
But people then just walk away from them full of spite.

You walk into the train station which is a common place
But your eyes are drawn to something unusual:
A man in a dress
Or at least that's your guess.
People stand and stare, giggling to their friends.
They point him out like he's a monkey in a zoo.

All this is clearly causing him distress
Because - in fact - he's a woman called Jess.

Now imagine this (give it a thought)
You're strolling through the park with your partner.
You just hold hands.
Until forcefully, in front of you a woman stands.
She stares at you and then your partner
And then whips out her phone and takes photos of you.
You think this would result in some form of bans
But instead she just gains more uneducated fans.

Now imagine this, (for a minute)
Someone you have no interest in asks you out.
You politely decline but they keep coming back.
Even though attraction for them is what you lack.
They still keep talking to you.
You feel you've lost your privacy.
You really wish they would just take a backtrack.
It feels like the whole world is turning pitch-black.

Now imagine this, (just for a second)
You walk into a train station.
For some reason people laugh and stare.
Why though you're unaware.
After all there's nothing odd about you.
You're just a normal person.
Are they looking at you because of what you wear?
You wonder why they even care.

You, your friends, your family, your school, your community
Everyone has a right to be themselves without the fear of discrimination.
Love who you want to love.
Be who you want to be.
Just always remember to respect others' lovers.
Just always remember to support who others want to be.
And something you have to do,
One thing you must:
Respect LGBTQ+.

Doctor Cheese

Him

As a child, like us all he was mad,
Football crazy, not slacking off being lazy.
The world was his oyster,
Hardly needing an occasional pointer.

After school he found new rules,
A job to provide and fill him with pride.
Years later, kids of his own would be here
Growing up content as could be,
Their dad an inspiration to them and me.

Now as a grandad he shows what not to do bad,
Them looking up to him as his own kids do and did.
He does anything for all, just give him a call.
He deserves a standing ovation, there's no need for persuasion.

Who you are or even however far,
Say thanks to the people that you can.

Isaac Fitzpatrick (13)
All Saints Catholic College, Huddersfield

A Design For Life

Let's build a house
firstly let's lay the foundations
now let's smooth the concrete
and let the excess run off like emotions
overflowing a human.

Next it is time to lay the bricks and mortar
let's start to build the frame
like building yourself up to do things
lift the wooden frames like our bones
and attach them into the ground

Also let's build the frame for the room
then start putting the underlay down for the slate roof
like our skin delicate, hardy
adjoining this is the insulation getting trapped

In before we lay the drywall to cover it
like we hide anger
now we will lay the dark oak varnished wooden floors
throughout.
We will attach our oak beams in the home then

Add the custom-made windows and garage doors
bifold doors front door and side door making it feel more
like a home.
Now we can get plumbing and heating put in
like we have our organs and hearts.

Thane Davenport (13)
Beech Hall School, Tytherington

The Amusement Of Sports Day

Dashing along the grassy path,
With all the parents with screams and laughs,
About to finish the tiring mile,
But hopefully in a flawless style,

Dashing along the grassy path,
The javelin's about to face the performer's power and wrath,
And as it travels through the clean air,
The performers are left in despair,

Dashing along the grassy path,
About to start the 100m sprint with a feeling of losing my breath,
And as the teacher says "Go!" there's a mixture of intense feelings,
But also have the feeling of wheeling past everyone with the headmaster greeting,

Dashing along the grassy path,
The sun is slowly setting, getting a compliment from the head of maths,
Running the relay with the last moments of the sun on our back.
And the next thing we know, it's pitch-black,

Dashing along the grassy path,
It's time for the awards, and we pounced our way back to school through the footpath,
And the feeling of winning a trophy, relieved the event is over,
Feeling like they have achieved madness.

Charlie Barnes (15)
Beech Hall School, Tytherington

A Pencil And A Pen

The lead of a pencil, the ink of a pen, the power of a pencil and a pen.
The roughness of a pencil, the fullness of a pen, the power of a pencil and a pen.
The pencil picks me up, the pen lifts me up, up, up I go...
Floating inspiration: I hope I make a great creation.
Touching the paper, starting to write, I can almost see the light.
The lead of a pencil, the ink of a pen, the power of a pencil and a pen.
Nearly finished, nearly done - but wanting to carry on, the power of a pencil and a pen.
A pencil gives you hope, a pen gives you a dream, writing is mine, I hope I finish on time.
The urge to write is so strong, I don't want to get it wrong.
Coming to the end of the line, and the end of time, follow your dream: I followed mine.
The lead of a pencil, the ink of a pen, the power of a pencil and a pen.
The roughness of a pencil, the fullness of a pen, the power of a pencil and a pen.

Amelia Semp (15)
Beech Hall School, Tytherington

Real Life

Do you think we get to choose where we are born?
Do you believe we pick the lives we live, like selecting a rose without thorns?
Do you think you suffer when you sleep all night on a comfortable bed,
While we rest our heads on rock-hard bricks and lie on stone-cold floors?
Every day one of us never sees the sun again,
And do you really believe that you are forlorn?

You go to private schools and learn English, science and maths,
while we are educated to fire a gun or take a never-ending nap.
When was the last time you went to bed hungry?
Do you ever stay up later than your bedtime?
Because every night we go out into the streets and sell food, so we do not start the next day hungry.

Daniyal Muhammad (16)
Beech Hall School, Tytherington

The State Of Things

Drowning under the knee of oppression
although this action unsheathes the truth
at the pinnacle of his aggression
alas we stand up and say, I can't breathe

women are repressed into a job
we have no name, just a label of you
told to clean or slave over the gas hob
more and more, we stand up and say me too

egomaniacs raging bloody war
waves of destruction in just one wee plane
running for miles, children starving and sore
we stand up and say I stand with Ukraine

imprisoned in our own homes like rats
lives taken away in a wooden cask
the deaths of our friends are set into stats
we should stand up and say, just wear a mask.

Harold Ghorbanian (15)
Beech Hall School, Tytherington

You Are You

Don't let people change who you are.
You are you and you're a star
People judge how others look
But don't worry
Look at the goods.
Always zoom in at the dos and the coulds
Never let anyone turn them around

Be the person you were born to be.
Don't let others say what you do.
Just be you, what you suit.
Cos no matter what you want to be.
I'm sure it will be the right thing for you.
As you are you,
And you get to choose.

Joel Wilson (15)
Beech Hall School, Tytherington

Tree

The tree is green and leafy,
The roots grow underground,
The big brown trunk
Is home to a skunk,

Sat in a branch was a big beastly bird,
How absurd!
Small birds nesting in a box,
Away from the fox,

A squirrel is finding acorns to stow away for winter,
Let's hope he doesn't get a splinter,
If I was up so high in the leafy loft,
I'd probably fall off.

Luke Francis (15)
Beech Hall School, Tytherington

Her Fault

It was her fault
It was her fault because she wore that dress.
It was her fault because she was walking alone.
It was her fault because she's pretty.
It was her fault because when she laughed she touched his arm.
Because her personal is flirty,
Because she didn't flirt
And we all know men love a challenge.
It was her fault because she looked good in ripped jeans.
Because her shoulders were showing,
Because her legs were out,
Because she didn't cover every inch of her skin.
It was her fault because society never taught her how to say no.
It was her fault because society never taught some men what the word 'no' means.
It was her fault because we have convinced everyone it is.
It was her fault because victim-blaming is the default.
It was her fault because she believes it is.
It was her fault because how could it ever be his?

Katie Bragg (14)
Birkenhead High School Academy, Prenton

Wasted

You are a tide pulling us under,
Wave after wave silencing our cries,
Forcing us to swallow the sand full of disgust,
Why did we destroy Mother Nature's trust?

Our lungs filling up with the bitter rage,
As we are left with nothing to say,
Our voice is drowned out by the thunder,
Now we are going down under.

Nature's course creating its own path once again,
Taking back what is rightfully theirs,
Now why should we class that as 'unfair'
When we caused it the despair?

We use too much paper,
Demolishing tree after tree,
But what else could we use
If it joins pollution's team?

Maybe give metal a go,
It's not harming any trees,
Yet it fills our skies with a horrid disease,
What difference does that make if it kills the bees?

The bees we need to pollinate our flowers,
To keep life in our grasp,

To bloom the fields of our concrete paths,
Why would we do this? Do we not think?

Another alternative is snatched in a blink,
What now? Why won't anything last?
Let's give plastic its turn,
After all it will last.

Oh but how wrong we are,
How blind we could be,
Plastic's not leaving,
It keeps our oceans bleeding.

Now look what we have done,
Extinguished what we were given for free,
How much more greedy could we be?
The countless stars will never be enough.

Bethany Cullen (14)
Birkenhead High School Academy, Prenton

Us

Floods, storms, heat,
Our planet is not the same
Extinction, drought, war
What is happening?
Famine, discrimination, deforestation
What's doing this to our home?
Us
Ice caps are melting because of our needs for cars, factories, indoor heating,
We're losing 10 football pitches worth of trees a minute
Just for paper we will bin, homes for livestock, palm oil
The ocean, our lands are filling will plastic, no room for their inhabitants
Plastic we will use once and then it is no good, no use
People forced to flee because their own homes and countries are not safe
Leave family behind for something that is not even their fault
Children starving to death, walking miles to get just water
Meanwhile, billionaires sit there in their one of five mansions
Animals leaving this Earth with no trace of ever existing
Other than the rugs of their fur, their ivory in china-wear
People hating on each other, causing pain and suffering to one another
And why: race, gender, sexuality, disabilities
What's become of this world?

Why are these things happening?
In the whole history of the world why now, why in sync?
Us
Us
Us.

Bethany Moran (13)
Birkenhead High School Academy, Prenton

Hope

Imagine your world was turned upside down
People you loved being moved around
The pool of hope about to wash away
With the people drifting far far away
But you still hope

You run till your last breath
Your legs about to take that last step
The thought that you have arrived
But no just one more mile but it might take a while
But you still hope

Your body begins to shut down with the fear you'll never make it
But in your head you know you have to commit
People in front of you helping others
Because they know they may only have each other
But you still hope

Eventually you see the light
The spark inside you shining bright
A sudden boost of energy
That this will only become a memory
And you still hope

When you make it to the border
Everything is in order
The smiles on everyone's faces

That maybe they have made it to safety
And you still hope

The past will forever follow you
But it will show how it changed you
How you have become a better person
From that thing that used to be a burden
And forever you still hope.

Charlotte Hilder (14)
Birkenhead High School Academy, Prenton

Her

Everywhere you go, you see her
She's in your dreams, screens, magazines.
Her perfect eyes
flawless lips
Her perfect hair
Flawless skin
You want to be her, but how can you?
You're not her, you never will be
You're so... different
Different isn't bad yet you can't make it seem good.

Society has changed us;
Changed the way we see, hear and think.
How did we let them drag us so far down?

Her face has been changed... but you already knew that.
Her blemishes, scars, spots, imperfections;
All taken away
Everything, that once made us unique now makes us grotesque.
Society took away our rights, our lives.
Are we really going to let them take away everything that makes us... us?

Her ocean-blue eyes follow you everywhere,
Her plump lips whisper in your ear,
Her snow-white teeth blind your sight,

How have we let them change our worth?

Katrina Skiba (13)
Birkenhead High School Academy, Prenton

Labels

What are labels?
Are they a promise that you are able?
Do they mould you? Shape you? Make you?

No. Don't you see?
They are anything but.
Labels are for the confused.

When scientists don't understand.
You are a novelty in the making.
When society can't see that,
When your god made you he said, "Ta da!"

Labels do not define you.
In fact, you are as free as a butterfly,
Fluttering and dancing in the breeze.

We are stars,
Burning brightly on a cool summer's night.
Can you see us? We are in flight.

What are labels?
Don't you understand?
When you are as rare as a snowflake.
When you're as beautiful as a star.

When society can't hold us.
They tell us who we are.

So wear your label like a badge,
Because you are worth so much more than that.

Phoebe Fielding (14)
Birkenhead High School Academy, Prenton

Women Empowerment

You may drag me down,
dig me into a hole you think I won't get out of;
but I will fight back.

You may pay me less,
take away my rights and make me alien;
but I will fight back.

You may say, "A man can do better"
but the only difference is gender.

Society is formed to prove a man is in charge.
That a man should do all the work, rule that family and be in power.

But what happens if you let a woman rule,
will there be no discipline?
Only love, jokes and children?

In the UK a woman has been in charge two times,
in New Zealand a woman has been in charge three times,
in the USA a woman has never been president,
what does that say about our world?

Ava Seabury (14)
Birkenhead High School Academy, Prenton

Doubt

This is for anyone reading or listening to this poem,
Who has ever doubted themselves;

Your abilities or agility
How smart you can be, how far you can go
Your place in society, your place in your family
Or even doubted their senses, or memory or morality

You're not alone, nor are you less than anybody else.

Everyone has doubts,
Some more than others
Your peers, your idols, your family,

Even your worst enemy

So it's best to not let these thoughts get to your head
Don't let doubts lead you misled
You can accomplish whatever you want
If you just let your heart follow a better font.

Philippa Davies (14)
Birkenhead High School Academy, Prenton

Who Is Normal?

There is no normal.
We all try to act like what we see on the Internet.
We think we are different to all our friends.
We think we need to be perfect but what is perfect?

There is no normal.
People pressure us, knock us down.
Everyone makes mistakes.
That is common.

There is no normal.
We can like the same things as people but that isn't called normal.
We can wish to be normal but what really is it?
We can compare ourselves to others but nobody is normal.

There is no normal.
Our hair and eye colour, our body figure.
This makes us unique.
Everyone is different and that's what makes us, us.

Taylor Lewis (14)
Birkenhead High School Academy, Prenton

You

You look me up and down with your laser eyes
You tear me down with your harsh lies
You make me feel uncomfortable with your stares and smirks
You make me squirm inside as you lurk

You film me with your phone
You wait to talk till we are alone
You move closer to me as I flee away
All I want to do is fade away

I cover my body and turn the other way
My body is not for your display
I cover my face
My body is not for you today

I should not have to cover up but I do
I should not have to change my clothes but I do
I should not have to hide myself but I do

All because of you.

Holly Wade (14)
Birkenhead High School Academy, Prenton

My Body, Your Body

My body,
My way, my shield, my weapon.
I have my body, you have yours.
If I wear shorts nothing distorts, the way I see myself.
Society can be hard, don't let yourself be scarred.

My body, your body.
If I am shy, don't expect me to suddenly soar and fly,
it takes time you see. You're you, I'm me!
I don't care about stretch marks!
To me they are sparks, sparks of confidence and charm.

My body, your body
Nothing is going to change this, you be you, I'll be me!
We may not have a happy ending all the time but it will be fine.
Make sure you don't lose your shine.

Villie Newman (14)
Birkenhead High School Academy, Prenton

Forgotten

Burning cities, destroyed homes, starving children
In a world which we call our home.
It may be far,
It may be a stone's throw away,
It may be happening to you right now
What matters is it isn't right.

Demons bombing a country because of conflict
Is that really going to do anything good?
People leaving their homes to seek safety
Why do we have to see this happen?
Why? Why? Why?

Poverty then takes over
Are we surprised?
What used to stand no longer remains
What used to live has a new home
What used to be is no longer.
Everything seems forgotten.

Awen Kingsley (14)
Birkenhead High School Academy, Prenton

It's Not Just Us

Animals suffer due to our actions,
just so we can have our satisfaction,
their lives are in a lot of danger,
just so we can game with a stranger.

Their homes are collapsing,
their food is being taken away,
what can we do to stop this,
how can we let this happen today?

We send bad gases into the air,
too fast for anyone to care,
but all the wildlife are being affected,
when really they should be being overprotected.

We have time to save them,
we can turn this around,
but we need to work together,
as we are in it altogether.

Ava Ryan (14)
Birkenhead High School Academy, Prenton

'Perfection'

The stress of perfection.
Media empowering us to change for the 'better'.
You look around when walking in the streets,
wishing you could be her or him meanwhile they may think the same thing.

These models are perfection.
In the chair they sit,
make-up being layered onto their face making them unrecognisable to loved ones.
But to the viewers online, it's their dream look.

Our elders are perfection.
They never missed due date.
They never cried or had friend issues and never got in trouble with their elders.
Why can't I be like them?

Teesha White (14)
Birkenhead High School Academy, Prenton

The Fiddle

I am the fiddle
They say they hear me but do they really?
I am the same as all the other fiddles, but because I make a different sound I am perceived as little.

I cannot change the way I am shaped, how polished or what type of wood I am
I cannot change the carves on my body or what brand I am
But I am still a fiddle.

I might be missing a few strings
I might not be able to make the same notes
But I am still a fiddle

I am still a fiddle, with tainted wood and carved lines
I am still a fiddle, why do I have to play the role I am assigned?

Ava Morrissey (14)
Birkenhead High School Academy, Prenton

The Boxes

Three boxes lie there motionless on a page
black
white
Asian
I hover for a second, figuring which one to tick
I think to myself, *if I tick white am I denying that my mother's heritage is pumping through my veins?*
But is it really that deep if I do?
But should my whole worth be put into a box on a page?
My family, my culture, into one small box
ticked away just like that
so I draw my own box just for
me.
as we all should:
a box just for you, and me.

Fatima Miller (14)
Birkenhead High School Academy, Prenton

You Will No Longer Win

To the person who once made me feel so bad about myself,
You will no longer win.
You can no longer make me feel like I don't deserve to be here like everyone else.
You won for a while.
Trust me, you made me doubt myself because of the way I was brought up.
But I have learnt that you just need someone to hurt.
Because your life is so boring you have nothing else better to do.
Well, you will no longer win.

Ella Gardner (14)
Birkenhead High School Academy, Prenton

Questioning Myself

Do I stand out from the rest?
Is my appearance noticeable
Or do I not stand out at all?
Do I blend in
Or am I different from everyone around me?
Am I the only normal one
Or am I the one everyone tries not to be?
Am I the laughing stock
Or is it someone else around me?
How can I change to fit in like the people who look down to me
Or am I going to be invisible to everyone else around me?

Bonnie Lovell (14)
Birkenhead High School Academy, Prenton

Our World

The seas are contaminated,
The animals are dying yet,
You still decide to contribute

What's a world without nature
And our environment,
Nothing, yet
You still decide to contribute

You've seen the warnings,
You're the problem,
You can help change things

Things for our health,
Our future,
Our world, yet
You still decide to contribute.

Molly Mason (13)
Birkenhead High School Academy, Prenton

Seek Out

Speak out,
and seek the help you need
take on the role as a lead

become the empowering role model you want to see
stand up for yourself, for you and me

take on the climb
as bright as you shine

stand up for what you believe
and become what you want to achieve

your voice shapes you
so speak up for what you want to see

speak out and seek out.

Seren Hulse (14)
Birkenhead High School Academy, Prenton

Reduce, Reuse, Recycle

Reduce the amount of electricity,
Reduce time in a car,
Reduce your plastic waste,
Or else we won't get far.

Reuse your plastic,
Reuse paper bags,
Reuse your clothes,
Turn them into rags.

Recycle your paper,
Recycle the wood,
Recycle your metals,
I hope you understood.

Reduce, reuse, recycle
These are words we all know and must now act on.

Emilee Crossley (13)
Birkenhead High School Academy, Prenton

Imagine

Imagine a world where everyone is free,
regardless of their race, culture, or nationality
a world free of crime, free of war, full of hope
a world where all people can live in harmony

Imagine a world where everyone has a voice,
no matter their faith, religion or beliefs
a world free of hate, free of fear, full of peace
a world where all people can be who they want to be.

Phoebe Lewis (14)
Birkenhead High School Academy, Prenton

Getting Older

I'm getting older.
My mother's loving ways
manage to get me through my lonely days
The smell of her perfume still brings back memories of happiness and pain
As I gain a candle to add to my crowded cake each year,
I slowly near the day I am able to leave this nest and fly high to my new life.
but I still need her shoulder
I'm getting older.

Niamh Cull (14)
Birkenhead High School Academy, Prenton

My Elected Music

In life there are some things that may annoy you,
But I still carry on when things are tough.
You are always there when I have nothing to do,
You bring euphoria through music.
But life must go on.

Some days if I am under the weather,
You harmonise whenever.
You make me feel as if I am at home.
But life must go on.

You are my universe.

Becky Wan (14)
Birkenhead High School Academy, Prenton

Run Free

We are trapped in our houses
while you run free

We cower behind safety masks
while you run free

We distance ourselves from our loved ones
while you run free

You have stolen the lives, hopes and dreams of all of us
and still you are allowed to run free

You have stolen everything from us
yet you, Corona, can run free.

Isobel Goodier (14)
Birkenhead High School Academy, Prenton

I Am A Woman

I am a woman.
Not to be told what I can't and can do.
Told that I don't have the ability to do what I want because I'm a woman.
That I am weak and don't have the strength to accomplish all my goals.
I am a woman.
Told that I can't have a say because my opinion doesn't matter.
I am a woman.

Lauren Hayes (14)
Birkenhead High School Academy, Prenton

Numbness

You know when you're numb
you just sit there
and doze off
into the distance
with a single tear, streaming down your face
no feeling or emotion
just silence
there's no anger, sadness or tears
it feels like it will never go
you're just numb.

Olivia Baker (14)
Birkenhead High School Academy, Prenton

Dear Me

Dear me from the past
I wish I said something when harassed
I wish I had that courage to speak
The times I felt meek

Dear me this day and age
I wish I did not feel this caged
I wish I didn't have to care
The times I watched them stare

Dear me time ahead
I wish not to hang from thread
I wish to protect my pride
The times I let it slide

Dear me any time
I wish to have a good lifetime
I wish happiness upon ourselves
The time I'll value my cover on the shelves.

Alexis Brown (13)
Chatham Grammar School, Chatham

Race Is Just A Word

My hair is as curly as a bowl of noodles
My skin is as brown as duct tape
I am not an alien
I am black.

Can I touch your hair?
No!
Just because my hair is curly doesn't mean it's different to yours
Just because I have an Afro doesn't mean I am having a bad hair day
Race is just a word.

Why do people think we are different because of our skin tone?
Race is just a word
Race is just a word
Race is just a word.

Why are black people seen by some as the cause of problems?
Why are black people discriminated against?
I have a dream that one day this world will change for the good
One can only dream.

My voice is a voice that should be heard and not ignored
I am no different to you because of my image

Race is just a word
Race is just a word
Race is just a word.

Deborah Adelaja (12)
Chatham Grammar School, Chatham

Bullying

Have you been hurt?
Have you been called names?
Have you been blackmailed?
Have you been assaulted?
Have you been neglected?
Have you been bullied?

But...
Have you been supported?

Bullying is like a stone crashing onto you.
Bullying is like a hammer breaking your heart.
Bullying is like a mental pain.
Bullying is like a knot in your stomach.
Bullying is like a feeling pulling you down into the abyss.
Bullying is like a nuke going off in your brain.
Bullying is like a virus affecting your emotions.

Bullying is horrible!
Bullying is nasty!
Bullying is disgusting!
Bullying makes you sad.
Bullying makes you feel down.
Bullying makes you upset.
Bullying makes you cry.

But...
Don't worry.
You have us.

You have your mum.
You have your dad.
You have your brother.
You have your sister.
You have your nan.
You have your grandad.
You have your family.
You have your teachers.
You have your friends.
You have your girlfriend.
You have your boyfriend.
You have your dog.
You have your cat.
But most importantly,
You have you.

Ollie Jokkrathok (13)
Chessbrook Education Support Centre, Watford

Beating Drug Addiction

Drugs are like a virus,
A computer that controls your brain and body.
A potion that takes control of your brain
Drugs are like we're in another universe.
Drugs are like you're fainting on a roller coaster.

Drugs make you feel like you are in an empty room,
Alone with no one there inside.
Drugs destroy social connections,
Drugs make family members cry.

You will become successful if you don't take drugs.
Your life will become stronger if you don't take drugs.
If you stop taking drugs you will have a good education,
Life will be as colourful as a rainbow.
All your dreams will come true.

If you find yourself having issues with drugs,
Be brave and talk to your doctor,
They can help and give you advice.

If you don't take drugs, you won't end up in a bad place!

Jack Jokkrathok (13)
Chessbrook Education Support Centre, Watford

A Tribute To The Lords

Having a family is the best,
When they come over I treat them as a guest.
Family is unique and always here,
Help me whenever I'm in fear.

Friends are not forever as they come and go,
If you're not careful they could be a psycho!
Be careful who you trust,
Loyalty is a must.

The ones I'm closest to are my sisters and mum,
We always stick together and have so much fun.
We like to dress up and hit the nail bar,
Bossing it out and looking like five star!

One day I'll have a family of my own,
And because of that I will never feel alone.
Hopefully I will follow in my mum's footsteps,
Always coming out stronger when I take a backstep.

Harmonie Lord (12)
Chessbrook Education Support Centre, Watford

Stay Positive And Be Successful!

Never dream about success,
Work for it.

Success is something you must work for.
Even if you have been for a long time,
You have to keep trying,
Cos one day you'll be victorious in life.

Being successful isn't easy to be.
But failing is not fatal.
Even if you aren't as successful as other people,
It's the courage to continue and to try your hardest,
That makes you fortunate.

Behind every successful person, lies a pack of haters,
When your haters see how triumphant you are in life,
They start hatin' on you because they never believed you would become a successful person.

Don't let anyone ruin your life and dreams!

Ricardo Da Costa (14)
Chessbrook Education Support Centre, Watford

Using Your Power

I always felt empowered,
But no longer wanted to feel like a coward.
Sometimes I'd cry when I was lonely,
And go to sleep slowly.
When I got home I wouldn't tell my mum or dad,
I'd just feel bad.

Just like Tupac said, "We all gonna die, we bleed from similar veins"
So why did these kids always make fun of me, thinking that I'd be in pain?

You must always remember you're never alone,
You should always know there's someone at home

There's always someone you can turn to for help.

Lucas O'Connell (13)
Chessbrook Education Support Centre, Watford

Life's Opportunities

Like Eminem said, 'You only got one shot do not miss your chance to blow'.
He means if you see a chance just take it and go,
Cos life may seem long but trust me it goes.
It goes quick you may trust someone and they abuse your trust
Then it turns out to be a trick.

After a certain time in your life,
You gotta do stuff yourself,
You gotta make things right,
No more teachers or parents to help you,
You've got to fight your own fight.

At first the realisation of life is truly a fright,
That's why you gotta take life's opportunities and win your fight.

Marcus Stipa (13)
Chessbrook Education Support Centre, Watford

Family

Family is number one,
Don't trust anyone.
They will always have your back,
Rolling in together as a pack!
When everything goes wrong we are all loyal,
At the end we are all royal.

Take every opportunity to celebrate life,
Never stab family in the back with a knife.
Find any reason to celebrate together,
We will be family forever.
Having my family makes me feel blessed,
When times are tough there's no stress.

Asim Babar (13)
Chessbrook Education Support Centre, Watford

Heights!

Heart racing
Out of breath
Amazing views of the night
Twinkling lights
Shining so bright
Not able to enjoy this moment
Scared for my life!

Keep challenging myself
Climb tall buildings
Climb trees
Go on a plane
Fight this disease.

Nothing will stop me
I can do anything I want
I won't be scared anymore
I have conquered my fear.

Bradley Hill (13)
Chessbrook Education Support Centre, Watford

Earth Is Getting Worse

The world is in a terrible place,
And we are running out of space.
Human population is on the rise,
People believe global warming is a pack of lies.

Earth's temperature is up 1 degree,
The land is going to be covered by the sea.
Forests will turn into ash,
The Earth is getting an insane rash.

Oliver Priolo Walker (13)
Chessbrook Education Support Centre, Watford

Year 7 Ends

As all of us Year 7s
Go on to be Year 8s
Now is time to look back
At the time spent with our mates.
It wasn't the year we hoped for
But we learned much, much more
Than sentences, algebra, and facts
Than science, English, and maths.
We learned what it's like to learn at home
And how to make sure we didn't feel alone
By keeping in touch on Teams and Zoom
By assemblies live from the living room.
Going out for our exercise daily
While the world around us was going crazy
We clapped on the doorstep for the NHS
And did are twice weekly Covid test.
Our teachers kept us all learning online
Our parents nagged at us all the time!
We made cakes and did crafts in-between more maths.
When school did eventually reopen
It wasn't quite what we had been hoping;
Held in a bubble
To keep us from trouble
Hiding our faces
And keeping to our spaces.

In December, family was kept apart
(Zoom quiz nights began to restart)
And Christmas ended up quite sad
The quietest we've ever had.
The snow arrived to bring us cheer
Feeling like maybe better times were near.
But it wasn't to be and the cases climbed
It seemed like 'normal' was far behind.
In the new year, school stayed closed
And once again we all stayed at home.
I missed my family and my friends
I wondered when would this all end?
But we have learnt to be strong,
To keep hope alive and keep going along,
And as the Three Lions roared
The hope of the nation soared and soared.
We will not be a generation lost
We are not the ones who will pay the cost.
We rise again stronger than ever
With this time written into our lives forever.

Niamh Ackroyd
De Warenne Academy, Conisbrough

Everyone Is Entitled To Equality

Equality.
What does it mean?
Being equal and deserving the same opportunities as others.
Everyone is human,
Don't treat anyone like an illusion.

No matter the colour of your skin,
Or if you're masculine or feminine.
Treat everyone how you would like to be treated,
Don't make anyone's heart defeated.

I hope my message has reached your head,
After all the empowering things that you have read.

Lewis Cox
De Warenne Academy, Conisbrough

Seed

I am a seed,
Seeds grow into flowers,
They blossom and bloom,
And grow as big as towers.

But I am only a seed,
Not yet reached my aim,
I am small, I am weak,
Overall, I am lame.

Though I am a seed,
I know what I will become,
And I will be limitless,
After time in the sun.

I will work hard,
I will grow into a flower,
Because, come rain or shine,
I know I am empowered.

Courtney Frost (13)
De Warenne Academy, Conisbrough

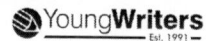

Empowered

E veryone gets that
M agical feeling that
P eople love them at least
O nce in their life.
W hen that happens,
E verything is perfect.
R ight there. Right then.
E veryone gets that
D esirable feeling that you are loved.

Jessica Johnson
De Warenne Academy, Conisbrough

Alight

You lit a fire inside her
As she was calling for help
Unsure what to do next
Igniting love for her true self.
Now she's alight
Because she did not surrender
Even though you never thought
A fragile little girl
Could burn as bright as the sun
And never be put out.

Hadassa Nkoue (11)
De Warenne Academy, Conisbrough

Blue

I have an amazing friend, Blue.
Yes I do!
She is always there.
She always cares.
When I am low,
She's never slow
To make a joke -
Folk might say she's like poison oak,
But when she's with me,
We're like two pods in a pea.

Minnie Jackson (12)
De Warenne Academy, Conisbrough

If I Had A Magic Wand

If I had a magic wand, I'd wish all my problems away.
If I had a magic wand, I'd make fun things last all day.
If I had a magic wand, I'd make everybody smile.
If I had a magic wand, I'd get rid of the rubbish piles.

If I had a magic wand, I'd create enough food for everyone.
If I had a magic wand, I'd get rid of all the machine guns.
If I had a magic wand, I'd destroy plastic.
If I had a magic wand, I'd make forests fantastic.

If I had a magic wand, I'd reduce the amount of carbon dioxide.
If I had a magic wand, I'd make sure people could enjoy the countryside.
If I had a magic wand, I'd stop global warming.
If I had a magic wand, I'd stop pandemics from forming.

If I had a magic wand, I'd make everyone in the world nice.
If I had a magic wand, I'd stop people melting the ice.
If I had a magic wand, I'd give you one too.
If you had a magic wand, what would you do?

Rebecca Rubin (14)
Dwr-Y-Felin Comprehensive School, Neath

Dear Future Me

Dear future me,
I hope you are thriving, living your best life
I pray that all your worries have dissolved to dust and there is no strife
You better be out there flourishing, making your great mark on the West End stage,
For I am working hard right now, so that you can earn a decent wage.
I wish with every ounce of my being that you have found who's important to you,
That you cherish them within your heart and keep them close when you feel blue.
I hope you've stayed sensible and not got sucked into any nonsense from others,
You've kept your unbreakable bond, hopefully, with your younger brothers.
We are distant, I know, myself and you
We are no longer one, but two.

In fact, that is why I am writing to you
To remind you of all we held true.
I hope you've found pride in every stretch mark, beauty spot and scar,
As that, my darling, is what makes you who you truly are.
Now you know enough to read between the lines,
Browse through my mistakes that felt like heavy rain from the sky.

I hope that the ghosts of the past have finally been set free,
And that they don't haunt you in the midnight air
The way they are haunting me.

Did you get some of the things that I've been longing for?
Answers, to the never-ending whys, why I'm who I am, I'm not sure.
Confidence, that isn't smothered by doubt and love, the indescribable,
The kind that I've only read about.
Are you embracing your every flaw, like you should be?
Judging people from what you know, not what you see?
Living life to the absolute fullest, your happiness bursting at the seams?
I jolly well hope you are following your dreams.
Remembering the life lessons you've been taught, putting them to good use,
Keep your friends and family close, don't become a social recluse.
My expectations for you are incredibly high
For I
Know that you
Will be true to your heart
Nobody will tear your ambitions apart.
Don't just survive,
Thrive.
Live the life you want to live with determination and grit,

I know and you know
It will be over before you know it.

Lily Williams (13)
Dwr-Y-Felin Comprehensive School, Neath

Don't Quit

Don't quit,
On the days where you see no highs,
Or on the days where there are no lows,
Whichever route you choose to take.
Don't quit.

Don't quit,
When things go wrong as they sometimes will,
When the road ahead seems all uphill,
When you're not being you, and life's a haze.
Don't quit.

Don't quit,
When the world seems against you,
When the whispers are a bit too loud,
When you start to crumble, while people push you down,
Don't quit.

Do you see the life ahead of you?
Do you want to live your life?
Do you want to get trampled on?
Whatever may happen,
Don't quit
Don't quit
Don't quit.

Daria Nita (14)
Dwr-Y-Felin Comprehensive School, Neath

Empowered To Be You

Girls like boys and boys like girls.
Being brought up like everyone else you see.
Nothing different you stick to the rules,
That's how they say it should be.

You're older now and everything's going to plan.
Until an unforgettable feeling arrives,
Until you look at a girl who you think is unusually pretty,
And you can't stop thinking of her eyes.

Girls shouldn't attract you like boys do.
Confusion and questions hurricane inside your brain,
You try your best to forget it, you scrub and scrub,
But this thought has left a stain.

Although not completely,
You finally accept the idea.
But no one can know or even suspect it,
The thought alone fills you with fear.

The men that get stabbed and the women who get bruised
You hear it on the news and on every radio,
They did nothing but love who they loved,
More than anything you want these feelings to go.

Rumours or speculation you don't understand how,
But somehow one day they all find out,

Every insult you know is hurled right at you,
Will you ever be normal? You start to doubt.

You lose too many friends,
Life has now completely shifted gear.
Suddenly you're not human,
Suddenly you're queer.

It's an endless and hurtful cycle,
Being tormented everywhere, even school.
But then a boy in your form class approaches you,
He says you seem quite cool.

The classmate is quick to befriend you,
He's a boy that likes boys.
You've never met anyone like you before,
It fills your weakened heart with all sorts of joys.

There are other people like you?
Finally you're no longer on your own.
But still in this huge frightening world,
To bullying you and the boy are prone.

It all continues to go on,
People scream slurs and splutter every mean name.
But now it doesn't seem like your world's crashing down,
Now your dignity is ready for you to reclaim.

You and the boy become best friends,
Feeling like a superhero duo as you brave the halls.

You ignore the people who strive to upset you,
Walking past them feels so powerful when you ignore their calls.

The feeling of freedom overwhelms you,
Bad thoughts and doubt start to disappear.
Suddenly you are a human,
Suddenly you're not just queer.

Jennifer Matthews (14)
Dwr-Y-Felin Comprehensive School, Neath

Teenager

I need a break.
Being a teenager all depressed and filled up with thoughts
Scared to fail exams and leave their parents distraught
Bullies' hearts are as cold as ice
Teachers never make them pay the price.

I need a break
I need a break

Trapped like a caged bird
Waiting and waiting for their voices to finally be heard.
Praying like a priest, hoping for some rest
Hearing the words 'exam' makes you instantly feel stressed.

I need a break
I need a break
I need a break.

Saul Otteson
Dwr-Y-Felin Comprehensive School, Neath

Pretty Girl

A society where you only
Desire me if my skin is full of life,
If my hair is long and luscious,
And my appearance is not welcome
If not decided by the many judging eyes.

You do not welcome me
Unless I have the build of a supermodel by the age of 12.
You do not like my body if it doesn't meet the expectations set by a male audience
For nothing but the objectification of my looks.

Why try to enjoy things if you deem me basic or a poser?
Why try to express yourself when there is a standard to meet?
But when you reach this standard best believe
It is your fault if anything happens because you are a pretty girl.

When did we change? Stop loving our bodies?
After all, you say beauty is seen from the inside.
We changed our love for women, to dictate their lives,
Only for you to tell us our use is useless.

So, venture out, get a job.
Even if that means your male counterpart is valued higher.
Because if you were a man, then you wouldn't worry.

The man is assertive, courageous, full of knowledge.
Not vulnerable, bossy, emotional and trying too hard.

In a world where my body is controlled,
We should take it back and love it all.

Stop the silence.

Speak up,
Love yourself,
Stop being sorry
For being the confident woman.

Sophia Mead (14)
Dwr-Y-Felin Comprehensive School, Neath

Dreams

The stuff of which dreams are made
In dreams,
My imperfections are absent.
Floating like distant thoughts no one can place.

Because
In dreams,
I live free from my own harsh standards
That watch me with judging eyes,
Criticising my every air and grace.

In dreams,
I walk through a meadow of spite
But the blades of cruelty don't pierce my feet
Or leave marks on my heart.

Because
In dreams,
I recognise my beauty, elegance, peace
And all the hatred I hold towards myself
Will slowly but surely depart.

In dreams,
My mind is laid bare,
And then,
Although in dreams I can be anything,
I choose to be myself.

Surprising,
After all the disparagement of my own character
I know that I'm
Perfect, free, enough.

Lily Mandale
Dwr-Y-Felin Comprehensive School, Neath

Trigger Happy

As he emerged from the shadows
I was indulged in fear
A gun in his hand
Staring at me as if I was mere

Our attention is on him
The villain amongst us
He laughs bitterly
In a complete muss

He knew I figured it out
The immense lie he had been hiding
I could feel myself shaking
The hatred I had for him was abiding

The air became silent
Tranquil and tense
My hand falters
It was all making sense

Trigger happy
That's what he was
A man with no morals
A man who's cold-blooded

His chapter is close to ending
His song has yet to be sung

He didn't have time to extend his wings
As he began descending.

Megan Cross
Dwr-Y-Felin Comprehensive School, Neath

Global Warming

Do you like the taste of plastic waste?
Neither do I
Stop
Stop throwing it away

Do you like the smell of the fumes
Coming from your fires
The burning of rubber tyres?
I invite you into my big swimming pool
But now you apparently rule
Throwing plastic waste into my sea
Most crucial animals you are killing, such as the bees.

Logan Lacey
Dwr-Y-Felin Comprehensive School, Neath

My Reflection

Mirror, mirror on the wall
am I perfect at all?
"No, no, no!
You're so fat
You're too ugly to even look at!"

Fat, fat, fat
repeating in my brain
it's such a shame I look this way

One day walking by
I felt a pair of eyes looking at my thighs
she came up to me
preparing for the heat
but...

"You're so beautiful!
And so confident!"
I couldn't believe this moment
"You will make so much progress
You're doing your best"

After that day
I wasn't so ashamed
all those thoughts devoured
I am empowered!

Eva Callaghan (12)
Fulwood Academy, Fulwood

The Sun And Moon And Man

Moon, moon glowing bright,
in the sky of the night,
covered in holes
as bright as a soul.

Moon, moon lighting up the night,
it smiles at the Earth.
As the sun rose
the moon's light froze.

The sun's light lit up the way
for the humans to destroy the Earth.

Man, man destroying Earth,
taking its resources,
wasting them straight away.

Wood, wood all of it gone
along with iron, gold and more.

Sun, sun burning bright,
lighting up the way
giving hope,
to those who have none.

Benjamin Fargher (11)
Fulwood Academy, Fulwood

Fighting

World Wars I and II were a place of death
World Wars I and II were no place for health
Barbed wire was sharp knives
Which horribly ended lives
Whistling bombs in the sky
This atmosphere would make you cry
Buildings falling
And families sobbing

It's 2022 our society's still fighting
Russia and Ukraine
Israel and Palestine
War comes running like a tide
Where shall they run? Where shall they hide?
For those who watched bullets fly
For those who are dead
And covered in red
We'll never forget.

Bouthaina Boutaine (12)
Fulwood Academy, Fulwood

Animal Cruelty

Don't abuse animals
How you would like it if you were abused?
They don't want to be reused.
To be made into fur jackets with their fur.

They don't wanna be scared because of you.
Life is frightening for those
For those who are stuck in a cage
For their whole lives.

Don't test on animals
Losing their lives just to test stuff
One by one animals go because of animal cruelty.
If you're going to abuse animals why get them?

Emily Bradshaw-Allen (11)
Fulwood Academy, Fulwood

Covid-19 Lockdown

Covid, Covid
Chaos was everywhere
Havoc and disorder
Healthcare to be found nowhere
There was no order

Covid, Covid
Working from home
Sanitising the post
Shops were closed
Majority prone
Minority immune

Covid, Covid
Nothing was left
Of life as we knew it
A new me emerged
A new us emerged
New communities emerged
We are *empowered.*

Mohammad Taqi (12)
Fulwood Academy, Fulwood

Love Your Body

Love the skin you're in
whether you're black
whether you're white
doesn't mean you don't have rights

Love the hair that you have
whether you're ginger
whether you're blonde
does not mean you are not strong

keep on fighting because you're great
your body is something you should not hate.

Be empowered.

Yuvraj Singh (11)
Fulwood Academy, Fulwood

The Dream

It starts with a dream
A drop of inspiration
One that never ended with someone's assassination
A ripple of the conventional starting a stream

It can take time, to build up pace
In modern-day times it's something we know
Equality is a wave starting decades ago
Proving everyone matters ignoring their race

Bad things happen to those who oppress
The ones whose acts are unimaginable, tyrannical
They can be tragic, the supposed death of democracy breaking into the capitol
After 58 years, just 15 minutes away January 6th storming of Congress

Sometimes a river has obstacles blocking the path
Deaths of the innocent going on with their day such as East 38th 25th of May
It doesn't have to end in pain and misery such as riding a bus exercising your liberty
Contributors to enforce the silenced billions' wrath

By the end of our time it could still be in motion
People have given their lives to push from behind
It's now our chance to sprint for the wire
Because eventually all rivers lead to the ocean.

Oliver Brewer (15)
Heathfield Community College, Heathfield

I Could Be...

It's not about 'I am', it's about what 'I could be'.
When you look inside yourself, is this what you really see?
See this person staring back at your reflection of empty space,
Someone who you admire and just cannot be replaced.
And in the bitter taste of sorrow they shine.
In a fault of a rock that is life they continue to climb.
When the harvest season is over and they still reap many more a crop,
For the sea only ripples when there's that tiny little drop of underlying hope that could remain locked up inside,
Bursts at the seams with everglowing pride,
Bursting, beaming, bubbling, bright,
So loud and proud it makes you jump with fright,
And it doesn't stop there, it continues to simmer,
For when you turn off the lights, there's always that small glimmer.
And when it tapers, it acts only as a store,
For the next large dose of empowered galore,
You think you couldn't even get any more,
But you do, and it's always been there,
Don't bottle it up, it's time to share
your experiences with others and provide inspiration,
Don't stop that train, it's nearly at the next station!
Then they'll soon be at the next destination,
Of hopes, of dreams, of motivation!

Do you realise now of the power you have to give?
To make the world a better place to learn, to live?
So it's not about what 'you are', it's about what 'you could be'.
And, when you look inside yourself, is that what you can see?

Alice Cronin (15)
Heathfield Community College, Heathfield

Women's Rights

How would you feel
Walking down the street,
Terrified about who you might meet?
Head flicking from side to side,
Trying to see who might be following behind.
Hands gripping at the bag on your shoulder,
And suddenly the area around you, getting colder.
And all you can feel is your heart in your chest
Just beating and beating and there isn't a rest

So how would you feel
If you were a woman
Scared for her life about what's going to happen?
Catcalling, abuse around every corner
Hoping someday that things would get warmer
But still the cold air around her just swarms her
Relying on that one person in front to warn her
She will never know what lies around the bend
But she is just hoping that this isn't her end

And how would you feel
When you just feel alone?
Whatever is in the future is unknown
And all you can hear are your mother's words
Be safe, be sound, and come straight home.
It is your first time out on your own,

You are a teenager, you aren't even grown
But you are still frightened for what is to come
And you don't even have support from your mum

How would you feel
Walking down the street,
Terrified of who you might meet?
We are women, children, elders, strangers
Unaware of the upcoming dangers
We should feel safe just walking down a street
Not terrified of who we might meet
So my conclusion from today
Is that the world needs to change, we were born this way.

Ellie Pascall (15)
Heathfield Community College, Heathfield

Just One

There is a word we all hear:
The word that is 'injustice',
You may know the definition,
'An unjust act or occurrence'
But is it just one?

There is a whole list I could say,
It can be counted on multiple hands
From race to gender to women's rights
It's a list that's just way too long
Is it still just one?

Discrimination against people of colour
Only just being recognised
By those higher than us,
The ones that control our lives
But it is still just one.

Being attacked for being gay,
Or having to fight for equal pay
There is too much to be said
We are aware of these issues,
But we still see it as just one.

Then there's climate change,
Younger people fighting for rights,
Rights to live.

Rights to breathe air that we don't own.
Yet it is still just one.

The cost of living going up,
Exams that stress the youth,
Mental health problems becoming normality,
It's seen as being 'over dramatic'
But no, it's still just one.

In a world where we just judge,
We could all just hold each other up
Instead of being divided through views,
Let's bring the light to the fact that it's not
Just one.

Aneshka Hunter (15)
Heathfield Community College, Heathfield

Though The Days Of Empires Are Gone

How can we say we've moved on
When we still put stolen antiques behind glass
Even though the days of empires are now gone
We still glorify the putting of slaves behind bars

Ripping children away from homes,
Sending them to a different land
Claiming they're savages who still play with bones
And saying it's fine because it's God's plan

Then we take their things,
And put them in a museum
Tell them we got it through a win,
Then we don't let them see them

We take their money
And kill their people
And force others to their knees
While we construct our steeples

How can we say we moved on
When we still blame them
Even though the days or empires are gone
We still hold their country's gem.

Owain Roberts (15)
Heathfield Community College, Heathfield

Phenomenally Me

Phenomenally me
I am a woman
Perfectly
I am me
Phenomenally

I am bigger than they want me
But I am happy being me
If I wear make-up I'm looking for attention
If I don't they make fun of my flaws

I get sexualised for my body
But when I cover up they won't see
The woman that I am
Phenomenally

I am a woman
Perfectly
I am me
Phenomenally

My stretch marks are like lightning bolts
Proving I can handle the storms
They told me to watch my calories
But they are batteries

No matter my size
I'll forever carry pride

As I stride
Through the cloud

I am a woman
Perfectly
I am me
Phenomenally.

Izzy Hearsey (13) & Leila Wort (13)
Heathfield Community College, Heathfield

Be The Best You Can Be

Everything ends,
Nothing lasts forever,
But, that doesn't mean that life is pointless,
Or that whatever you do will affect nothing.
It's the opposite - you can make a difference,
You can be the best at whatever you want to be.
The only thing that's stopping it is you...
You need to get up when you're pushed down,
You need to make the best of a gloomy day,
You need to look at the glass half-full.
But, most importantly you need to promise yourself something,
Something important,
Something that you need to follow, every day of your life.
It's 4 words and 4 words only,
Have a brilliant life,
But, this doesn't mean you just live a brilliant life.
You need to radiate your joy and brighten other people's days,
And you need to help anyone who needs it,
All I am trying to say is,
That your life means something, and you should make it the best life you can possibly have!

Ethan Buckley
Hungerhill School, Edenthorpe

Embracing My Leadership

Time has flown, it's that time of year,
It's a celebration, it's a time to cheer.
Memories have been made, uniforms have been signed.
Exams are now over and now there is peace of mind.

Year 10s have seen their fate and I know what is to come.
Our duties must be fulfilled, before our time is done.
Unique personalities, competing for the roles.
Running for student leadership, that is my goal.

I want to make a difference, I want to be like him,
I want to lead the school proudly, for that I need to win.
I hope my wish comes true, I'm nervous all around,
In order to succeed, my confidence must be found.

Will I make the right choices or end up causing harm?
Communication is not my strong suit, but I must unwrap my abilities.
I think that I can do this, I think that I will be fine.
Once I become a student leader, I will learn over time.

The polls are now in…

YES! I have been chosen and now I'm part of The Team
I can't believe this has happened; it's always been my dream.
I let my passion show and I gave it my all,
They saw I could handle anything, no matter how big or small.

There is no time to relax, wipe away my satisfaction
Determination is key now, I've got to start the action
To make the school a better place by listening to the voices.
Silenced. Stifled. Suppressed. They're dependent on my choices.

I am making a difference, I am being me,
I am leading the school proudly, for everyone to see.
My wish has now come true, I am no longer afraid
In my pursuit, I have found success and someone bolder has been made.

Time has flown, it's been a wonderful year,
It's a celebration, it's time to cheer.
My term is now over, the new journey has just begun
Extending this advice to you, before my time is done:

"I have experienced what you have experienced,
I know what it is like,
Now it's time for you to take your place
and transform this new community."

Yu Qing Huang
Hungerhill School, Edenthorpe

Hypocrisy

Not far from here,
Faint panting can be heard
Heavily muffled but distant.
Not far from here,
Bombs plummet to the ground.
Not far from here,
Asylum seekers from Afghanistan try to seek refuge; but are turned away mercilessly...
Not far from here,
Young girls like Malala Yousafzai are deprived of educational rights and shot when resisting to obey unjust commands.
Not far from here,
People from Ukraine are getting immediate attention from the media after bombings.
Not far from here,
Refugees who continue to struggle, for a far longer period than those in the media, are getting no help and are getting sent to Rwanda
Please tell me,
Are their screams not enough?
What will it take for their plight to finally be recognised?
So please tell me,
Why the double standard?
When did it become so blatantly biased in this world?
When did it become so easy?

To stop the public seeing the mass destruction that has been caused to asylum seekers' homes.
When did it become so easy to help people from Ukraine but, not other asylum seekers who have been suffering in silence for years?
When did it become so easy, to turn a blind eye to modern concentration camps in China?
When did it become so easy, to be so cruel and heartless?
Not far from here,
Is a little girl in pain. Cut. Stitched. Ironed...
Crying to be heard because she is taught she is nothing.
She is taught she will never be more than a wife or a mother.
Taught that she is another person's property.
She could be your sister or daughter...
Do you want that future for her?
Or do you want to stop it?

It's your choice...

Ameenah Din (12)
Hungerhill School, Edenthorpe

Losing Yourself

Losing yourself
It's been 2 years Nanny,
I still don't understand why,
Why this had to happen to you,
You were my best friend,
Now you can't remember.

It's been 3 years Nanny,
I still hate to see you as you are,
Laid in a bed trapped,
In a continuous loop of torment,
Tormented by memories.

It's been 4 years Nanny,
It's not the same without you,
I remember every Christmas,
When you came around to celebrate,
But now you can't remember.

It's been 5 years Nanny,
I know you don't have long,
Hold on for me, please,
I've already lost you once,
I'm not losing you again.

It's been 6 years Nanny,
I still hate going to see you,

To see you laid in a bed,
Losing yourself,
But I can't help you.

Chloe Nesbitt (13)
Hungerhill School, Edenthorpe

Medieval Thoughts

I thought it was 2022 until you made that comment.
I thought you were respectable, educated and 'one of the good ones'.
Your thoughts are medieval.
You are evil.
With each sarcastic comment like your own,
You rip me apart like pulling wallpaper out of your childhood bedroom, which you wouldn't understand
It is obvious you haven't grown up yet.
But you see,
I'm like a snake.
Shedding is part of the process,
Because with each unveiled layer I am bolder, brighter and harder to ignore.
My drive for success and my dreams are constantly driven over, stamped on and left for nothing constantly
Because of people like you;
Holding society back in the 1400s.
Unless you have a time machine, it's time to move on.

Mia Wilson (13)
Hungerhill School, Edenthorpe

We Are The Light

We are the light, that burns red and orange with rage,
As it untangles and unravels itself,
Consuming everything in its path, and we think:
This land is God-given, why shouldn't we take it?
Nature is fragile, why shouldn't we break it?

But when will we realise?
That the bark we burn isn't just wood?
It's armour. Protection. Skin.

And the greenery we blacken
Isn't just scenery?
It's bright. Thriving. Living.

So, we are the light that flickers yellow and white
With hope, as it untangles its past
And maps out a path, for our future, and we think:
This land is God-given, why can't we embrace it?
Nature is fragile, so shouldn't we save it?

Lilly Ryan
Hungerhill School, Edenthorpe

Sitting There, Waiting

Sitting there, waiting
For someone to speak
Sitting there, waiting
For someone to accept me

"I do accept you completely"
They all say
They hide it discreetly
That they don't care to say

They all say
"Sorry if I hurt you
But I don't care
You are different
So we will leave you in despair"

"Of course we accept you
We are all different
Of course you're beautiful
Of course you are significant"

Sitting there, waiting
For someone to speak
Sitting there, waiting
For someone to accept me.

Kacey Compton (12)
Hungerhill School, Edenthorpe

Bringing Back Them

War is made by boys but fought by men
War is leaving people behind and bringing back them.
Shell-shocked and afraid, as they are wheeled back with holes too deep to comprehend.

These boys were not men
But these men are now boys
Fighting a war for men but hurting boys.
The boys are sat while the men stood
Regret covering their bodies with mud.

Loved ones sat at home waiting for their hope
Men sat in hope waiting for their homes,
'We need you' but you don't need them
Blue-eyed shadows the pain.
But the boys will get their eventual gain.

War is made by boys but fought by men
War is leaving people behind and bringing back them.

Grace Hobbs
Hungerhill School, Edenthorpe

The Pandemic

How did we suddenly go from good times and sunshine to inside and online?
'Stay safe' 'two metres away'
Wondering if it would be okay.
'Normality' became a term we weren't used to hearing
Hoping these cases would start disappearing.
Locked inside, lots on our minds.
Searching for new recipes and whatever else we could find.
Not even four months in
And our lives were in a spin
The constant never knowing of how and when this would end...
So our lives could begin to mend
Families kept apart
Coping mechanisms becoming the new type of art
2020 was never our friend

Will the pandemic ever end?

Ashlea Rawlings (15)
Hungerhill School, Edenthorpe

I Will Always Love You

Sometimes all I want to do,
Is turn around and talk to you.
To wrap you up in my arms,
To keep you from harm.
I just want to show you how much I love you,
But saying goodbye was the hardest thing I've been through.

You may have been ready to go,
But all I could do was scream no.
I wasn't ready.
My heartbeat unsteady.
Crying was all I could do,
Because saying goodbye was the hardest thing I've been through.

But now you're in a better place,
And you will not be replaced.
You can run free,
Soon things will get easy.
I will always love you,
Because saying goodbye was something I had to go through.

Sasha Lilly
Hungerhill School, Edenthorpe

Global Warming

I hate to see the ice disintegrate,
So many species lose their habitats,
This issue is not really very great,
I wish the world could just shut up and change!
If we do not change soon it will be too late...
Then, our world will get to its fatal end.

Think of the polar bears that will perish,
Would you really want that to happen?
So many people will perish too.
The world is heating up quickly,
You can help to stop this issue.
So, will you just sit down and ignore us?
Or will you stand up and make a change?
Come on and help us tackle this problem.

Riley Lowcock
Hungerhill School, Edenthorpe

Perfection

I have made many mistakes,
because I am human.
I will never be perfect,
I will only imperfectly try to be.
You can buy a bouquet,
you try to find the 'perfect' one with no flaws with every detail on point
You won't find the perfect one
Let your heart accept the imperfections,
accept yourself just the way you are.
Sometimes the most special people are the ones who are beautifully broken,
To be honest it is not how you look on the outside.
It's based on your personality inside.
No one is perfect
you need to accept who you are.
You can't expect everyone to be perfect
I don't understand why people try to be 'perfect',
We are perfect in our own special way.
everything and everyone has imperfections,
I was once also trying to be 'perfect'.
You can't be perfect just accept it.
If we were perfect nothing would be new and we would know nothing else apart from the expectations.

Anna Kwan (11)
Kingsford Community School, Beckton

Because We Want Our Voice

Everyone's had that time where they had an excellent idea,
One that would change everyone's life, but couldn't vocalise it.
A superb concept, wasted away because no one would listen.

But these facts and statistics are being thrown at us and reiterated.
But what's the point?

Stated in the Bible, James 2:17, 'what are words, without actions?'
'What's the point in knowing but not doing?'

We, the young generation, are being silenced.
Our voices are being imprisoned in our minds.
We're treated differently,
As if we're different kinds.

We drown in pain, they tell us to train
Although we've been slain.
But we've spoken so many times that it's becoming a crime.
Everyone goes through stress
To the point we yearn for darkness.

Some of us end up in red pods
And seriously now how have you not learnt from Mr Goole?

They say we're sly,
When we always cry
But why?

But... why?

Thuvaragan Yogeswaran (15)
Kingsford Community School, Beckton

Tell Me Why?

My heart is loving yet people hate
Through ignorance others discriminate
For our colours are seen as a threat
And left behind like a silhouette
Must people always petrify
No one can ever tell me why?

I walk in the street and people glare
and clasp their bags in great despair
They tell me, "You people don't belong here!"
They tell me, "Must your kind always interfere?"
And though one heart may become so wry
But no one can ever tell me why?

For we stand and shout with our desperate voice
Yet unrecognised crimes have left no choice
We battle on blood, sweat and tears
Thus still people aren't sincere
My swollen eyes look up to the sky
And beg for you to tell me why.

The colours of the world must unite as one
For the Lord's our shepherd and we His son
This message for the world forever sent

For these challenges are quite frequent
May those among us never cry

For soon someone will tell us why.

Shafiqar Namuwaya (12)
Kingsford Community School, Beckton

Powered Love!

Love...
Once you feel it
You will never need to know
That love completes the feeling
... Onward... upward...
We grow.
You will never think to yourself,
Should I look for another?
Love is what we need...
Just ask your mother.
Do we love anymore?
Can we love anymore?
Do we love despite the flaws?
Am I a complete mess?
Without that special feeling
That I get inside my chest.
Can we love with other issues?
Don't you know, love is best?
If we strengthen our core
That's where our love lies.
We must embrace it.
Without love, dry my eyes.
Something so perfect
You'll never want to leave it.
Love someone quickly

And never feel defeated.
Find your love...

Gracie Steward (12)
Kingsford Community School, Beckton

No One Is Perfect

This is life, we all think about it twice.
The things we do and the things we say will always be
a surprise.
We try to make it perfect and try to make it right.
But there is no such thing as perfect
and there's no such thing as right.
We always think of the perfect marriage,
the perfect wife, the perfect job and the perfect life.
We are all human, living a human life, everyone so different
and unique in their own way.
So why can't we be who we really want to be
And stop being this perfect
person everyone else wants us to be?
Do your best, be your best.
There is no such thing as perfect, so take a rest.
Be happy.
Be free.
Not perfect.

Gabija Surovec (14)
Kingsford Community School, Beckton

Have Black Lives Ever Mattered?

Rosa Parks gave us freedom on the bus
The doctor was our spokesman and the boss
Maya Angelou was an activist and wrote the lot

We breathe the same air, but their air gets squeezed
Because of the colour of our skin, just like George Floyd
"I cannot breathe"

Black is black
White is white
Life is always a racial fight
Sometimes life isn't fair
In every shade of colour, there is beauty to be found
There are differences to admire, but through the human race we are bound

It's not black versus white
It's about doing what's right

Stop the hate, it's a sin
Until then, black lives matter.

Aisha Salim (12)
Kingsford Community School, Beckton

The Real Idol

Idols.
They're the ones that we see on a screen,
we see them as kings or queens.
Sometimes it is how it seems
but most of them have that habit of deceive(ing).

We view ourselves as little and weak
while we view them as kind of unique.
But, when their reputation creaks,
they get hate messages within a week.

Sometimes though, their perfection gets to us
and we try to act like them thus
we start to lose our own trust
as we look upon ourselves in disgust.

But you need to understand that the true idol is within you.
Voice it out into existence and you will truly see the lion in you.

Obinna Azu (14)
Kingsford Community School, Beckton

Women Are As Strong As Men!

Men say a woman can't do work
they are housewives
looking for a man like a damsel in distress,
but us women
are not weak
we are strong
and brave
and have rights.

She is a woman,
a mother, daughter, wife, sister
and has a great job.
She is strong and smart.
She has a brain and
knows how to use it.
She is talented and has hope and beauty.
She has respect and love for you.

She is as strong as a man
maybe even stronger.
Be strong.
Be smart.
Be you.

Don't say you can't before you discover you can.

Arpita Hossain (12)
Kingsford Community School, Beckton

Free

Stretch your wings and fly
To places unknown
Where you may sing your songs
And know that you belong

Dance in the wind and the sun and the rain
Live each day like your last
Reveal your exceptional beauty to the world
And don't dare look at the past

Spring heats up and summer falls
Winter takes the light away
Yet here you stand, proud and tall
Your hope will never fray

And I could sit here all day long and stare at the sky
Wondering if the birds wish they could be as free as you and I.

Nazmia Njie (15)
Kingsford Community School, Beckton

Women Against Racism

M any risked their lives for equality
A n activist she was
Y ear by year it stays the same
A nd she never gave up

A gainst racism
N ever did she give up
G ave her all for peace
E quality is what she wanted
L ove and hate many fought
O ver everyone she was admired the most
U p and down, over and out, was there equality after all?

Sheka Hamdoun (13)
Kingsford Community School, Beckton

A New Year, By Kiril

The snow swells,
The crowd quells.

As the fireworks flare up,
Everyone's one year grown up.

'O' blessing, 'o' new year,
To people enlivened to drink some beer.

Must everyone feel happy,
when the sun is out sunny.

Good fortune to start again,
When people can gladly entertain.

When people can only say goodbye,
They sadly begin to cry.

Kiril Kazakov (12)
Kingsford Community School, Beckton

Take That Step For Yourself!

You are free in this world of ours
We are the change
Just be yourself
You do what you have to
There will be challenges but you need to keep on going!
Life has challenges, but that's natural for everyone
Believe in yourself and that is your way to your success
Failure is a word but not what lets you down
Just accept the things that put you down
And let it go
Your happiness is on its way.

Rajveena Kaur (12)
Kingsford Community School, Beckton

Life As We Know It!

During this modern time in society
It's quite hard to live by
Making everyone feel a surge of anxiety
Almost to an urge to cry
We have diseases, wars, crime
Thousands of people die
In fact, it happens all the time
Sadly it's not a lie
Life as we know it
Not always as clear as the sky
Life as we know it.

Daniel King (12)
Kingsford Community School, Beckton

Ugh Homework!

Homework, homework, homework
Oh how I hate homework
One of the worst things on Earth
It makes my head hurt
It's useless, it's pointless
It always disappoints us
On the weekends we're meant to play games but instead we're consuming Headaches
Homework, homework
Homework
Oh how I hate homework!

Yannick Castro (13)
Kingsford Community School, Beckton

Vigour

With our vigour and might
To go against all odds
To make it right
Keeping goals in sight

Always remarkable in life
To radiate high and bright
To obtain vitality and fortitude
All wishes for delight and a victorious habitude

To build steady trust and evolve
To flourish with the hope for all.

Iris Bagga (12)
Kingsford Community School, Beckton

Acrostic Poem For Special

- **S** uper kind
- **P** layful and never sad
- **E** nergetic and confident
- **C** omical
- **I** ntelligent
- **A** rtistic and creative
- **L** ikeable and popular.

Taqrim Arabi (13)
Kingsford Community School, Beckton

Everything Falls Into Place

I stare, enraptured by the way you move -
drifting your feet so delicately across the lacquered stage.
Even with the odd stumble or misplaced step back
everything falls into place.

You project your words with such emotion -
even if you don't have much to say.
It's crazy how repeated lyrics that heal hearts,
help everything fall into place.

You probably don't know me -
but many people know your face.
I'd like to thank you always and forever,
For helping me find my place -
Because you helped me discover my rhythm -
and angle my glance,
to realise -
That the steps backwards which repeated themselves,
were all part of the dance.

I hope to grow like you -
to completely find my feet,
no matter what it takes.
Although sometimes I'm confused -
and don't know how to feel -
I just remember that in time,
Everything falls into place.

Scarlett-Jane Hart (14)
Lathom High School, Skelmersdale

Monday Blues

Monday,
Monday I get your blues,
I get your blues on Tuesday,
I get your blues on Wednesday,
I get your blues on Thursday,
I get your blues on Friday,
I get your blues on Saturday,
I get your blues on Sunday,
It's an endless cycle of your blues,
Your blues trap me in my own mind.
When can I escape?
Your blues are meant to stay in Monday,
But your blues bled into Tuesday,
Your blues bled into Wednesday,
Your blues bled into Thursday,
Your blues bled into Friday,
Your blues bled into Saturday,
Your blues bled into Sunday,
There is no escape.
You let an endless black cloud hover over me,
I wonder if it ever ends,
Will your blues ever stay in Monday?
You can't dismiss Monday blues
Because it's just like something stuck to your shoes.

Emily Clegg (15)
Lathom High School, Skelmersdale

Hello, Can You See Me?

Hello, can you see me?
It's quite easy.
I stand out a lot with my dark brown locks.
Can you see me?
Can you at least hear me?
It's like time just froze,
I'm stuck in this sad dark pose,
I want to feel free,
Oh I just want to be me.
But no one likes the inner me,
That's the part they can't see,
At all.
My heart is broken,
Like dismembered rock,
Or a set of china.
I'm lost like a puppy,
I'm as sweet as a child.
Most of all,
I'm really fragile.
I know what it feels like,
I know it doesn't feel right,
I just want people to see me,
People to hear me.
I feel as though I'm a lost ghost,
I only hear people through the post,

Claiming things with dark notes.
Can you help me?

Jessica Morgan (13)
Lathom High School, Skelmersdale

Not One Love

Men and women
Women and men
Love has no meaning or boundaries
Love can be anywhere:
Family, friends and relationships.
People can hate
But what if you have found your soulmate?
There isn't one love
No there is much more
If you found the one
Don't let people tell you different
They are the one you love
Don't listen to people's opinion.

Millie Evans (14)
Lathom High School, Skelmersdale

Dear Future Me

Unyielding I stand in the midst of the fray,
Unbound by the chains of society,
Unperturbed by their stares, their smirks and their snorts,
Unafraid of insecurities that hide within.

With grace I march through thistle and thorn,
With courage I endure a barrage of malice,
With dignity I denounce all evil in my way,
With honour I strive to protect my pride.

Now is the time to confront our demons,
Now is the moment to end our mistreatment,
Now is the chance to begin our climb,
Now is the opening to face the fire.

Embark on my journey to change the world,
Embody the tenacity and own the show,
Embrace your wildest hopes and dreams,
Empowered. That's you and me.

Rashed Hussain (14)
Marriotts School, Stevenage

Decade

As you're stuck in bed,
In the same circle of life
The dark thoughts consuming your head
Cutting your dreams like a knife
You hope this to be different in a decade
Life is a devil lurking
Reading to rip your dreams
You just have to keep working -
And stop defeat bursting at the seams,
You hope this to be different in a decade
Age 13 and 1000 problems in
You have dreams to have kids, travel, drive
Somehow you never feel you can win
Have you lost the energy in life where you thrive?
Teen break-ups, floods of tears
Deepened anxiety, pressures of school
Things have got so hard over the years,
But you still have to live, this is a rule
It's not so easy though -
You hope this to be different in a decade
It's a decade on,
The sun has replaced the forever rain
That resembled your pain,
As the dreams you wished whilst you slept
Came true as you took the plunge and leapt

Smile across your face each morning
Giddy kids and a husband you call mine,
Looking forward to new days dawning
Knowing a decade on, life is fine

That person you used to be
No future, feeling lost
You got your dream, now feel free
You could've given up, but at what cost?
You used to say I hope
Now you say I will
If you feel like giving up
You say nope!
So your life doesn't come to a standstill
Grab life with each hand
Achieve all your heart's desire
In a decade life will be grand
As the unique person within
Begins to transpire
Use all inner strength,
For the future
Stop, I hope this to be different
In a decade
And know -
It will be different in a decade.

Phoebe Henry-Beattie (16)
Marriotts School, Stevenage

Make Your Own Story

Never a wait for a Prince Charming
To wake you from your slumber.
Snow White made that mistake
Never sacrifice your treasures for a man
You shall regret and feel imprisoned and not in control
Ariel made that mistake
Never leave your glass slipper behind
Marry for love, not because a prince believes your looks are majestic
Cinderella made that mistake
Never live your life in fear of curses and the bad
Be free, have your own destiny as curses shouldn't ruin you
Aurora made that mistake

Don't wait to be woken up
Wake yourself up

Be like Elsa
Bold with power, confidence and authority.
Be like Mulan
Strong, wise with a will to fight until victory.
Be like Pocahontas
Adventurous, kind-spirited and a peacemaker.
Be like Merida
Independent, recognisable and brave.
Most importantly, be yourself,
Pick up that pen and create your own story and your own legacy

Life is never a fairy tale
Don't be a princess; be a queen.

Emily Bartosik (13)
Marriotts School, Stevenage

The Colour Of My Skin

Oh, the colour of my skin, the colour of my skin.
Everyone wishes to judge;
Just by appearance without any interference,
Without a fair chance but looked at with a momentary glance
Some polite yet others not so polite
So many stereotypes just for a particular genotype...
The quiescence of unique, dazzling flowers
Solely due to the misuse of God-given powers.
When will the world be equal, when will the world be true?
So many religious beliefs but where is the virtue?
Misjudgements, assumptions, accusations occurring every day
Has God really created life to be this way?
Looked at with a misleading grin just because of the colour of my skin.

Oscar Gonsalves (17)
Marriotts School, Stevenage

Now It's Time

You've had your ups and downs
You've had your smiles and frowns.
But now it's time to spread your wings and turn your feelings around.
You've had your good and bad times.
You've had your past but now it's your prime.
But now it's time to think about yourself before your heart divides.
You've had your family there for you.
You've had them there when you're not feeling blue.
But now it's time to come around and do what you want to do.
You've had your time of sorrow and pain.
You've had your time to run away.
But now it's time to gain your strength and not to play the same game.

Lexi Morley (12)
Marriotts School, Stevenage

Red Teddy Bear

I miss my teddy that fur so soft I was always warm
But my carelessness made me cold
I miss my teddy I miss her too
As my doll sat in my room I couldn't help but cry
As my teddy was miles away, probably with another kid
I miss my teddy but maybe if I had only looked back
It would still be with me today
But it's gone now and all that's left now is its heart-shaped pillow
I miss my teddy and I feel so sad
I can't believe I left it on that bus
But I guess I will be more careful when I leave somewhere
To avoid the same mistake from happing again...

Cleo Iftime (11)
Marriotts School, Stevenage

Dear Future Me

Dear future me,
One thing I want to ask you,
However bad things get, keep going,
And try again

Dear future me,
I ask you one thing,
Don't be afraid to ask a question
Even if you think it's stupid

Dear future me,
I ask you one thing,
Don't be afraid to cry
Everyone does it at one point

Dear future me,
I ask you one thing,
Reach out to the people that love you,
They love you too

Dear future me,
The last thing I ask you,
Is to be yourself,
If people don't accept you for who you are,
Then they are not the right ones for you!

Sky Newman (14)
Marriotts School, Stevenage

The Key

If you want it done, do it yourself.
Why wait, when you can do it?
Go out there and show them how it's done!

But when I, the girl, am confident,
I am too mature for my age,
I am the reason the boys in my class are so rowdy,
I am asking for it.

But when he, the boy, is confident,
He is a leader,
He is powerful,
He has his life under control.

How can he be empowering,
But I am headstrong?
How can he be confident,
And I, cocky?

They tell us,
Confidence is key.

But the key belongs to him.

Tiana-May Redford (14)
Marriotts School, Stevenage

Fear

Fear is here,
Fear is nigh,
Fear resides in everybody's eyes.

Mould it, shape it,
Make it new.
Create the power to break through.
Shape it new and make it yours,
For now, you can heal your sores.

When darkness falls,
Let fear be a fool,
Bravery is your greatest tool.

Gouged and gashed and drained from rage,
Let it scream in its untimely cage.

When the moon shines brightest,
As do you,
Never forget that hidden voice inside,
That speaks true.

Riley Dale (14)
Marriotts School, Stevenage

When...

When will you stop hiding in the shadows?
When will you sing with no fear?
When will you dance with no shame?
When will you show yourself kindness?
When will you say what you want to say?
When will you live without limiting yourself?
When will you be unapologetically you?
When will you burn the brightest you possibly can?
When will you realise the answer is now?

Jessica Parker (14)
Marriotts School, Stevenage

Let's Live In Peace

For many years they were slaves.
Doing as they were told, living in fear.
Many years later they were finally treated as equals
Let's hope history does not make a sequel.

Now in 2022 all lives matter
But for the longest while black lives didn't matter.
No matter what anyone's colour or creed.
Let's continue to live in peace.

Lauretta Sylvester (14)
Marriotts School, Stevenage

Empowered, A Confident Me

I take deep breaths and breathe
To build me to be stronger and allow me to grow.
I'll wait and be patient and things will get stronger
My confidence will grow and mature and make me more powerful.
A confident me.

Theo Milburn (12)
Marriotts School, Stevenage

My People, It's Time

The money drops deep as does my school.
I never walk, 'cause to walk is my family of tool.
Beyond the walls of empowered, life is defined.
I think of rappers when I'm in a school state of mind.
Hope my fuel gives me some sense to not fool.
My mind don't like school.
It's all about rules and it's getting too cruel.
In a school state of mind.
What more could you ask for? My time? The empowered?
You complain about life.
I gotta love it though
Gossiping about me just makes me glow

School just entertaining and boring, like a job
Boy, I tell you, I thought you were a blob.
I can't take the life, can't take the empowered.
I woulda tried to sleep I guess you is just a coward.
In a school state of mind.

Oliver Goodenough (15)
North East Surrey Secondary Short Stay Unit, Hersham

Let's Get It

Life is going right and ain't going to be getting stab by no knives,
Just waiting for my time to strike.
Not like Russia tho ain't trying to cause no World War Three,
I'm just trying to make my paper and leave.

I know I might have been an underachiever,
But this time I ain't gonna be stopped,
You never know you might just be little shocked.
Anxiety got me stuck but I'm going to make to the top.

I am just trying to get my voice across,
Also know and heard everybody say they from the same place,
But they do know the hurt and pain,
And the mental issues that go on inside the brain.
But this anxiety really got me stuck.

But one day we will be winning and ain't no doubt about that.
This year is all about myself,
Might sound selfish but I've had too many backstabbers around.
You know since early I've been naughty kid,
Mucking about and getting kicked out school,
Isn't the way to go because you will lose hope.

But you lot just wait I'm going to flip script,
My main focus is to turn losses into lessons and get more wins.
And this is where it should begin,
Also I'm going to let out the beast that is within.
But one thing you lot should know, is never forget where you was born and grown.

My family are the ones I owe everything to,
Without my mum around I would of drowned.
Glad she didn't die when I was younger because without her I would have been a goner,
But this anxiety has got me stuck.
Wait till I'm older and I've moved my mummy out that council house.
I hope she is proud of how far I've come,
I hope she don't give up on me like all the other mugs.

You know if you achieve you will believe,
So let your eyes and vision see,
You can do anything if your mindset's free.
So don't let anxiety kill everything you're destined for,
And don't worry Nan I know you're looking down from the stars,
I will heal from all these battle scars.

I ain't going to let this anxiety get me stuck no more cause I've grown from the war,
I've been battling with myself and I'm starting to see the light.

Freddy Johnson (16)
North East Surrey Secondary Short Stay Unit, Hersham

The Day Ahead

Just woke up 8am in my bed,
I've been blessing the day ahead,
Praying that I don't end up dead,
I think I should get up and leave my bed,
Shawty's telling me she wants link me,
And go and make some bread,
Shawty's stressing me out,
Got me sat here shaking my head,
Just woke up 8am in my bed,
I've been blessing the day ahead,
Praying that I don't end up dead,
I think I should get up and leave my bed,
Shawty's telling me she wants link me,
And go and make some bread,
Shawty's stressing me out,
Got me sat here shaking my head,
I've been sat here before,
Why can't I win this bloody war?
People chatting on my name,
But I'm just pushing for the fame.

Emilia Wall (13)
North East Surrey Secondary Short Stay Unit, Hersham

Pizza 'N' Chinese

I would get on my knees for some pizza 'n' Chinese,
Hopefully it comes at the perfect degree,
I'm hoping I get some prawn crackers free,
Though I don't like the delivery fee.
Need to order that pizza; don't want that coming at three,
It's gonna cost me some serious p.
Can't wait to see all the extra pep'roni there'll be,
I would travel the sweet and sour seas,
For the best pizza 'n' Chinese.

Kenny Campbell-Smith (14)
North East Surrey Secondary Short Stay Unit, Hersham

Change

You can't win, you know you're weak,
You won't make it, you're weak
You can't live like this, you're weak,
You can change, just not yet,
You will make it, you're getting stronger,
You can live like this, you're strong,
You are power-hungry, stop!
You are changing for the worst, quit now,
You can't be helped, I'm sorry,
You've lost control, wake up!
You might not get another chance.

Harrison Gianni (14)
North East Surrey Secondary Short Stay Unit, Hersham

Empowered

E nable your change to understand language,
M ind can cause you to be blind,
P ushed into pressure,
O ppression from the police,
W orking hard for nothing,
E ntrust is difficult,
R espect is necessary in the world to have a good life,
E ntitled people around me,
D ominated by the people in my life.

Nathan Brown (13)
North East Surrey Secondary Short Stay Unit, Hersham

Love

Love is special
Love is pure
Love is true
Love is magical
Love is one of a kind
Love is unique
Love is amazing.

Sophie Robinson (14)
North East Surrey Secondary Short Stay Unit, Hersham

Firefighters

Fire alarms go off,
The firefighters respond.
They go down the pole,
And grab their gear.

They go out to save lives
They go out to the rapid flames
They don't play around
They get everyone out

Heroic people, never in doubt
They fear their lives
They put themselves in risky positions
Rescuing off cliffs, vehicles and buildings.

This personality of helping people
And kindness is who I am and
Who I want to be: a firefighter.

Jack Pearson (15)
Orion Academy, Blackbird Leys

Gym Etiquette

Gym etiquette
Out there at the gym,
Pick up the weight
You are stronger than you think
And then you blink.

You think this is easy.
Then you realise you'll never rest freely.
Until you get your results
And then you'll see clearly.

Squatting to the moon
You'll hit that PR soon.
Bench press the weight
It is worth the wait.

A bet against the mirror
You'll never miss the old self
Only worrying about my health.
Because it supports my wealth.

A journey to Rome,
'Cause this is what you're doing.
And Rome was not built in a day,
So neither will you.

While everyone else is messing about
At parties around the streets

You get yourself together
And chase your dreams.

Caden Watts (15)
Orion Academy, Blackbird Leys

Dear Female

Dear our daughters,
The world is bright.
You may not see it yet,
But it's a charming sight.
The opportunities are endless,
But the stigma is still there.
Girls can get angry!
Let's make these things fair!

Dear our young women,
You're the famous path.
The one where you find yourself,
Whether it's music or it's maths.
The choices are endless,
Though stereotypes can scare.
It is your body,
Let's make these things fair!

Dear our mothers,
I admire your care.
There never is despair,
Even if mayhem is there.
The solutions are never-ending,
Though those questions cannot be beared.
It doesn't matter who 'wears the pants' in the family!
Let's make these things fair!

Dear our women who do not want children and will not be told that they have to by anyone,
It is your life.
You will not be known as a potential mother,
And without children you can still be a wife!
Your decisions always matter,
But the controllers are (but shouldn't) be there.
There is nothing wrong with you!
Let's make these things fair!

Dear our grandmothers,
You're our leaders of the pack.
The guru of the family's females,
The power of all the hacks.
Whether your pudding, pies and basketball
Or chess and solitaire,
(or both!)
You are still strong and puissant!
Let's make these things fair!

Lola M
Outwood Academy Ripon, Ripon

In Their Steps

I read about Anne Frank and her family, using books, as they are the best source,
And the treacherous betrayal by a Dutch informer, without guilt or remorse.
Their traumatic story starts in Amsterdam, with a Jewish family of four,
Hiding with four others, in a sealed-off area during the war.
After the cowardly betrayal, they were transported from the secret annexe,
To Auschwitz in Poland, a massive concentration camp complex.
At least they were together, this small comfort was to be short-lived,
The Frank girls, Margot and Anne, after seven weeks were moved.
To Bergen-Belsen a notorious death camp, where they both died within days of each other.
The only one to survive their traumatically sad story was Otto, their father.
In April a few weeks after their tragic demise,
Bergen-Belsen was liberated by the Allies.
I wish to visit these places, I'm unable to properly explain why,
I realise this emotional trip, will definitely make me cry.
The Franks' personal story is now a part of history that will endure and last.
We must not forget, but learn from the atrocities of the past.

To walk in their steps and know Anne was there,
Is my way of remembering and to show that I care.

Ruby Fielding (12)
Outwood Academy Ripon, Ripon

I Should Be

My poster said I should be strong,
But I lost my arm.
My poster said I should be a hero,
But no one wants anything to do with me.
My poster said I should be happy that I survived,
But all I feel is guilt.
My poster said I should be brave,
But all I wanted to do was go home

In the trenches...

I should be at home but here I am,
Shooting innocent people,
Against my will,
Causing devastation.

My love should be in my arms,
Not my metal ones.
My love should be in my hands,
Not in my metal ones.

These men should be okay,
Yet they're depressed.
These men should be happy,
Yet they are petrified that they might be killed.
These men should be at home,
Not in the trenches.

Will they accept me?
Will they want me home?

Jasmin W D (13)
Outwood Academy Ripon, Ripon

I Should Be...

I should be out there seeing flowers, girls and sunsets
But instead I see blood, guns and hail
My boss said I would be a hero
But everyone acts like I'm a zero

I thought this would be fun
But this is my own hell
I would normally be sad if I lost someone I love,
But I'm used to it by now

I used to go to sleep full and happy for my next day to come
But now I'm starving and scared of what's going to happen next
Am I going to live or am I going to die?
If I don't survive, then goodbye

Will I make it to tomorrow?
If not my family will be full of sorrow
I wish I never came here
I wish that I had stayed
At least then I wouldn't have to go to sleep at night and pray to live another day.

Ashley Collins (12)
Outwood Academy Ripon, Ripon

Time

9pm:
I put down my shattered watch
Not long now I think
Not long now

Mere hours ago they said I would be fighting
Fighting for glory, fighting for victory
For the empire
Now I lay here in this dreaded ditch
Half my leg missing but I feel no pain
Only the sharp sting of the cold on my skin

10pm:
Surely they will soon come for me?
My brothers, my battalion
Do they not care for this lost soldier?
Do they not care?

As it appears they do not.
They do not.
For they have left me sitting here to rot.

Myles Wainwright-Baker (13)
Outwood Academy Ripon, Ripon

I Should Be

I should be powerful
but I am weak
I am scared
I am weak

I should be proud
but I am shameful
I am guilty
I am shameful

I should be home
but I am at war
I am in a trench
I am at war

I should be normal
but I am broken
I am ill
I am broken
Was it worth the years in hospitals and institutions, nurses smiling at me with pity in their eyes?
Was it worth the pain of war?
Was it worth seeing my friends die before my eyes for a sliver of glory?

Was it worth it?

Shaneequa Aryee (13)
Outwood Academy Ripon, Ripon

Empowered With Sadness

Everyone eventually comes to death,
Reaching their last gasping breath,
That happened to Bella, my rabbit,
Being risky was a habit,
Her cage was open and she ran away,
Only to be a fox's prey,
Bella and Twinkle were never found,
That made my happiness fall to the ground.

Twinkle was white, Bella was grey,
I haven't seen them since that day,
Twinkle was my brother's bunny,
Both probably in the fox's tummy,
I feel like a rubbish pet owner and a fail,
I miss their cuteness and their bunny tails.

I can't believe this happened to my bro and me,
It all happened so suddenly,
This really saddened me and my fam
Empowered with sadness, yes I am...

Bella Boo
And Twinkle too
I love and miss you.

Olivia Jayawardana (13)
Plume, Maldon's Community Academy, Maldon

Anxiety

This poem is all about,
The anxiety people face throughout
Sadly it's a common thing,
To have this wretched curse within.

It can show at any time,
Even when the sun does shine
Hide it away you might say,
Keep it from others until it's too late.

But that is not the way to go,
Anxiety is okay you know
Never hide it to yourself,
The quicker you tell the faster you'll get help.

Anxiety only makes you stronger,
Even though you may wander
If this wretched curse will go,
That you will never truly know.

How do I know how it feels? you ask,
I've suffered from anxiety long into my past
Some people have it and some people don't,
But it doesn't make you different and believe that it won't.

Use it to empower you,
To make you succeed

Believe you can get through it,
One day you will be freed.

Harrison Monk (12)
Plume, Maldon's Community Academy, Maldon

Woman Of The Moon

The moon would stare back at my gaze,
an angry glower of luminescence dismayed upon its face.
I imagine a woman there;
cradled in the embrace of a crater,
or perhaps ruling this lone planet in mere empowerment.

For a woman may keep the heavy tides of wrath and indulgence at bay,
thus keeping the waves of atmosphere away from a planet we have yet to stir down;
as our very own has been reduced to but oceans of dissatisfaction.

Keep a white flag in the soft, ashy ground,
fond woman of the moon;
so we may see you have surrendered to the planet within its beauty.
You are the moon to its very core,
protect such delicacy with the strength of your mind alone.
Keep our mortal hands resisting from your tormenting success.

Lois Kingsford (14)
Plume, Maldon's Community Academy, Maldon

Time's Running Out

Tick-tock, tick-tock
That is the sound of a clock.
Its hands go round and round.
Never-ending, tick-tock

Tick-tock, tick-tock
The Earth, a giant ball of rock.
It spins round and round,
Waiting never, tick-tock.

Drip-drop, drip-drop,
The slow melting never stops.
A bear walks round and round,
Looking for help, drip-drop.

Tick-tock, tick-tock,
That sound needs to stop.
Our lives keep going round and round
But not for long, tick-tock.

Paddy O'Brien (14)
Plume, Maldon's Community Academy, Maldon

Them And Us

They have Guns, but we have Flowers,
They have Hatred, but we have Love,
They think we have Fear,
But we have Confidence.

Everyone is the Same,
But Different.
They have Pain and they Use it,
We have Pain and we Change it.

Molly Welsted (15)
Plume, Maldon's Community Academy, Maldon

Girl's Mind

I never really liked the way my body looked,
the grease in my hair, the oil in my skin and the gap in-between my teeth.
I never really liked the way my body looked,
the way I fitted into clothes, the way my hips dipped.
I never really liked the way I looked,
I got into modelling but not in a good way,
looking up to them,
wishing that one day I would wake up and look like one of them.
Then after a while, I saw models just like me,
with gaps in their teeth and hip dips.
I never really liked my body,
but seeing other people be empowered with features like mine
showed me that it's *my* body and nobody else's.

Rihanna Williams (11)
Poltair School, St Austell

Family

Family is life,
Family is support,
They will help you through the toughest of times,
Even when you're at your lowest points in life,

Family is life,
Family is support,
If you're lost in a world of fear,
Looking for an answer,
They'll always be there to help you,

Family is life,
Family is support,
When you fail or fall,
They'll always be there to pick you up,
Dust you off,
Comfort you,
And help you start again,

Family is life,
Family is support,
Be nice to them,
Be kind to them,
Because family,
Is everything.

Lill Durham (12)
Poltair School, St Austell

Earth

The Earth, the miracle that keeps us alive.
The Earth, the home of wildlife, the creator of life and all that lives.
The Earth, our home, our birth-giving, but if we destroy it what will we have left?

The Earth, our home, if we want to keep it we have to pull out of the darkness
Endorse new ways back into the light.

The Earth, thank you we deserve to pay you back for all the good you have done for us
Thank you, together we can make things right so those with ideas don't be afraid to share.

Lucas Hart (12)
Poltair School, St Austell

I'm A Teacher For A Day

Dear future me,
I'm a teacher for a day,
I like maths
I love English,
All the students hate English and maths!

I send some students to horrible removal.
I give all my fantastic friends merits,
I send teachers home because they're excluded for a month,
I send the head teacher to removal because he is absolutely annoying.

I tell everybody to do revision,
I tell them to check it,
I tell them to write full sentences,
I tell them to do it in silence!

Jacob Wells (11)
Poltair School, St Austell

I'll Be Here, You'll Be There

I'll be here
You'll be there
If you look up you will see me in the air
Whilst you're sitting on a chair,
Down there.

So if I'm here
And you're there
Where is here?
And what is there?
Did you see that thing in the air?
Now there are lots of them up there.

But I'm here and you're there
In the sky so big and bright, up there.

Why can't you be here with me?
Not in the air, up there.

Rhianna Smith (14)
Poltair School, St Austell

Balloons

Humans are like balloons,
You can kick them,
Punch them,
And even beat them up,

You can bend them,
Twist them,
Or stick them on a wall,
But they won't pop,

Little by little,
Every act is weakening them,
All it takes is a little bit of pressure,
And then,

Pop!

The balloon is broken,
Ready to be discarded,
And forgotten about,
Buried away,

Never to be seen again.

Phoebe Jones (13)
Poltair School, St Austell

Family

Family are for life,
I will never use a knife,
They are always there for you in hard times,
If you feel lost just remember they love you.

Family are for life,
I will never use a knife,
They always love you,
Family save you at your lowest.

Family are for life,
I will never use a knife,
They try their hardest,
For you.

Family are for life,
I will never use a knife,
Be kind,
To the people you love.

Ellie-May Hockaday (11)
Poltair School, St Austell

Alive

I feel most alive when I'm surfing,
skimming through the water and watching the waves flicker like a candle.

I feel most alive when it snows
and the snowflakes drift from the sky and cover the ground like a blanket.

I feel most alive playing cricket,
boom the sound of hitting the ball boosts my adrenaline.

I feel most alive when I'm with my pets,
their face is a magnet and I'm drawn to their cuteness.

Molly Wharmby (12)
Poltair School, St Austell

Summertime

Sun shining in the sky,
Children laugh and rarely cry,
Little ones play among the grass,
Where barbecues are made fast.

Beach days are a perfect way,
To spend the holidays,
The gentle shore splashing against the bay,
People laugh and children play.

But it will soon come to an end,
It will grow cold and windy.
People will hide and wrap up warm.
But summertime will come back around again.

Hollie Wheat (12)
Poltair School, St Austell

Journey

Our destination is a place,
So much bigger than we know,
For some the journey is quicker,
And for others slow.

'Life is like a camera,
Focus on importance,
And capture good times',
For some day you'll complete your journey,
And get to where you need,
Just try your best,
And then you'll succeed.

Anastasija Truskovska (13)
Poltair School, St Austell

Pride

Thank god for boys.
Thank god for girls
Thank god for humans
In this world.

Boys can like pink
Girls can wear blue
Your reaction
Is up to you.

When someone's proud
Let them be them.
Let boys be girls,
Let girls be men.

Don't hate because they're different
As that's not up to you.

Grace Quinn (12)
Poltair School, St Austell

The Wand!

It brings you everything you wish for.

But be careful because all isn't good,
it could change your life and it will never be the same.

You don't want this going into the wrong hands,
it will bring you consequences.

If you are lucky it will stay with you,
and you will continue to have good luck.

Chloe Owen-Walmsley (12)
Poltair School, St Austell

The Buzzard

Its wings steadily ripple through the wind as it sits staring, waiting for prey.
Then it spots something.
Gone.
It had to keep this decadent reward at bay.
Those deep empty eyes see every part of Cornwall
From abandoned tin mines to unlevel moors.
You may wonder what bird this is
Well the buzzard of course.

Leah Rapson (12)
Poltair School, St Austell

Dear Future Me

Dear future me,
I want you to believe in me,
Because I'm a teacher for the day,

Dear future me,
Do you remember me,
When I sent everyone away from me?

Dear future me,
I hope someone else becomes the teacher of me,
For the day.

Lilly Morcom (12)
Poltair School, St Austell

War Is Hell

W alking
A round me
R ough bullets

I nside their heads
S lowly walking

H ell is around me
E verywhere around me
L ying around me
L iving is worse than dying in this hell.

Jack Stanhope (12)
Poltair School, St Austell

Harry Billinge

To the man who saved our lives,
I shall pray every night.

To the man who was willing to sacrifice his life,
Knowing he was about to lose his wife.

To the man who was fearing the worst for his mates,
We were all there to pray.

Klea-Ava Spiller (11)
Poltair School, St Austell

Empowered

I am worried about Jota
I am worried about Ukraine's war
I am angry about Rangers beating Hearts
I am angry about Putin taking over and killing innocent people
My concern is the world
My concern is the future
I am hopeful that Celtic win the league next season
I am hopeful that the war will stop
I am inspired by Liel Abada
I am inspired by brave people in Ukraine
We have the chance to win many games
We have the chance to help people
I know that we are the best
I know that we have a chance to be better people
I am empowered by Celtic winning the league.
I am empowered by the people of Ukraine.

Neil MacRury (12)
Sgoil Lionacleit, Isle Of Benbecula

Climate Change Has To Be Sorted

I'm worried about climate change
It has been going on since the 1800s
Polar bears, losing their homes
Unbearable temperatures
Sea levels rising
Storms, fires
It makes us feel sad, horrible
As if there's nothing we can do...

But we can
People can have a say
Feel empowered
Try and stop climate change
Put up posters, change to renewable energy
Don't use fuel-powered transport as often
Join or run clubs, make plans, ideas to save the planet
All these things are going to make a huge change
And it all comes down to people like
You

The wonderful places in the world
Are in danger, and could be gone in years to come
All because it wasn't sorted years before

All us people have to do is know
We are powerful, and can make a difference.

Feel empowered, and don't listen to the people saying
"You're wasting your time" or "What's the point?"
Because the point is
It's for our planet
And us empowered people
Are going to save it.

Allan Smith (13)
Sgoil Lionacleit, Isle Of Benbecula

Climate Change

Seasons are changing
Weather is crazy
Wind and rain take hold as each day arrives.

Lots of destruction
Animals suffer
Newborn animals hide from gale-force winds and fierce sounds
And the sun's powerful rays
Which are burning like fires
Too much rain floods the ground

I hope the future improves as people change their habits
And the weather will start to be kind.

The ozone layer is changing, people need to be aware
Not to leave a legacy of pollution
But to make the air cleaner, to help the planet breathe.

Patricia MacDonald (13)
Sgoil Lionacleit, Isle Of Benbecula

Climate Change

Ice is melting, animals are dying
Struggling for food
Magnificent creatures starving
Putrid plastic piles with revolting rotting rubbish
Do we have 50 years?
Will there be unbearable floods?
Will bees still be around?

Maybe it's not too late
Maybe we can change
Do we need all this plastic?
All this rubbish and energy wasted
Maybe we can live without it
And in peace...

Erin Steele (13)
Sgoil Lionacleit, Isle Of Benbecula

What If...

What if all the ice caps melt,
and the Earth floods?
What if the world goes into a drought,
and we have no food?
What if all the animals
die of heat, and starvation?
What if we die?
What if in a few years we have no planet...
But...
What if we stop wasting food?
What if we recycle more?
What if we walk or cycle to more places?
What if we stop this nonsense?

Naomi Menzies (12)
Sgoil Lionacleit, Isle Of Benbecula

Pearl Of The Orient

Glooming prophecies creep through our minds,
Wiping out our only eternal light with tear gas and water cannons.
Ruthlessly tearing our trust away from the police,
The dawn never showed up...

Praying to be alive,
Under the cloud of depression and darkness.
The pearl is bleeding yet it's covered with lies,
But the guardians of our only conscience have gone gently into the night.

Attempting to obstruct our only chance,
But the void to veil can't control our destiny.
From the catastrophe we slammed our doors,
Upholding our original aspirations we never surrender.

Morphed into the water we flow,
Flooding the world with our spirits we stand up again.
Come alive! The truths don't lie!
And the dawn finally came...

Aston Wong (15)
St Peter's Catholic School, Surrey

The Gracious Ones

Angel choirs sing endlessly at the gate.
Our Lord waits patiently for broken ghosts,
to uplift them to reach eternal fate,
and he then becomes our all-loving host.
Break free from chains of our forgotten past,
parted from the confinement of our earth.
Unfilled bones remain, when we breathe our last,
as we await our spiritual rebirth.
However, memories of you live on.
In the minds of the ones who truly love.
Who pray for you to the Lord God upon,
amongst God the father and gracious ones.
You will be remembered for all of time,
many lost souls will find peace within thine.

Conor O'Riordan (14)
St Peter's Catholic School, Surrey

Esoteric Grace

She was made of dimensional glass.
Those who loved her could see from within,
The fairness that were the flowers that grew in the botanical beauty that was her.

Others would see her with hatred,
With words of despair and destruction,
Calling her a monster and broken.
Shattering the glass until there were only fragments of what was her.

If only they had looked past the reflection.

Veronica Delgado Barrios (15)
St Peter's Catholic School, Surrey

The Phoenix Prometheus

On a farm with other slaves
Tied and chained on a hot day to do forced labour.
Scattered, separated, estranged;
Picking cotton, waiting to be saved.
Waiting for this, our daily suffering, to end.
Backs sore, seared by rays of light,
Tired and lightheaded,
Our souls and bodies numb;
Whipped from day to night, perennial
Perpetual, unending suffering prevails.
And yet,
Beyond that farm with other slaves
Lies a world with no more ties and chains;
No labour, no anguish, no pain.
Instead a vision rises to meet me;
A hope burning bright as the searing sun;
A vision to end all suffering -
The prospect: peace.

Julian Rampaul
Taunton School, Taunton

Beneath The Mask

Under the mask hides a soul
Minus the one thing that makes it whole;
Afraid of things others might say,
People's words stuck on replay.
Overthinking.

Tired of keeping it all inside
It's time to stand again with pride.
The you of the past has long since died;
Now is not the time to hide.
Move forward.

And now, leaving the shadows far behind,
Long out of sight and far out of mind,
You hold up your head, put a smile on your face
And feel empowered.

Ema Petkova
Taunton School, Taunton

Mistakes

We feel it every day
No matter what or where
You will always feel pain
But that doesn't mean you need to be scared
You will learn and grow
From trial, error and mistakes too
You will get better and know
That mistakes empower you
Over and over again,
You may be knocked down
You may fall and drown
But keep moving forward
Because what doesn't kill you makes you stronger.

Carlton Chu (14)
Taunton School, Taunton

Take Control

Take control,
Believe in your words,
Have confidence in you,
Break the chains that hold you back.

Stand up
For what you believe,
Believe in yourself,
Don't let anyone put you down.

Hold firm
To your dreams,
For if dreams die,
Life is a barren field, with a dark grey sky.

Be yourself,
Let your personality shine through,
Don't be afraid,
To stand out from the crowd.

Tom Middleton (14)
Taunton School, Taunton

YOUNG WRITERS INFORMATION

We hope you have enjoyed reading this book – and that you will continue to in the coming years.

If you're the parent or family member of an enthusiastic poet or story writer, do visit our website **www.youngwriters.co.uk/subscribe** and sign up to receive news, competitions, writing challenges and tips, activities and much, much more! There's lots to keep budding writers motivated!

If you would like to order further copies of this book, or any of our other titles, then please give us a call or order via your online account.

Young Writers
Remus House
Coltsfoot Drive
Peterborough
PE2 9BF
(01733) 890066
info@youngwriters.co.uk

Join in the conversation!
Tips, news, giveaways and much more!

YoungWritersUK   YoungWritersCW   youngwriterscw